Falling Bodies

Falling Bodies

Andrew Mark

G. P. Putnam's Sons
New York

G. P. Putnam's Sons
Publishers Since 1838
a member of
Penguin Putnam Inc.
375 Hudson Street
New York, NY 10014

Library of Congress Cataloging-in-Publication Data

Mark, Andrew.
Falling bodies / by Andrew Mark.
p.   cm.
ISBN 0-399-14447-1 (acid-free paper)
I. Title.
PS3563.A6623F35   1999   98-33261 CIP
813'.54—dc21

Printed in the United States of America

3   5   7   9   10   8   6   4   2

This book is printed on acid-free paper. ∞

Book design by Gretchen Achilles

For Kelli,
who believed

Acknowledgments

My gratitude to Andrea Simon, Laurie Liss, and Leslie Gelbman for their enthusiasm, tenacity, and sound editorial advice. Thanks to Scott Brenner for his fine-tuning of my physics. And much appreciation to Garry Bliss, JRP, and DRP for their always encouraging words.

I shall never believe that
God plays dice with the world.

ALBERT EINSTEIN

Falling Bodies

Prologue

The handwriting was hers. He had known when he opened his mailbox, but he made himself wait until he sat down before he read the postcard. As was his habit, he took a table near a back window overlooking the narrow, cobbled street of warehouses and meat packers. He got himself out every Wednesday night, came here when the restaurant was quiet. He liked the feel of the streets downtown, slashed by steel trolley tracks that broke through the worn asphalt, and on some nights, slicked with a bluish rain. The restaurant had no sign outside, in fact, he wasn't even completely sure it had a name, but it was comfortable and bright in a warm way. Being here made him feel less like some solitary creature of the night.

Maybe it was called Plant 609, but he really didn't know for sure. Stamped on a bronze disk sunk into the concrete floor by the entrance were the words EUREKA BATTERY PLANT 609. He imagined the vats of greenish acid and tanks of shimmering mercury and rolls of steel. But all that was gone, and all that remained were great iron chains and tracks that ran across the ceiling to move heavy equipment. It didn't really matter what the space had once been, buzzing with charging devices, crisp with the smell of ozone. It still served the same purpose as far as he was concerned—eating and charging batteries both initiated chemical reactions.

The tables were brushed stainless steel and the light fixtures were caged and industrial. The interior was red brick, with high vaulted ceilings and wide leaded windows that let in the bleached street light. A waitress set his beer on the table and took his order: grilled salmon and crisp fried potato puffs.

It seemed that all the time in the world had passed, and that none had passed at all. His routine had drawn him so deeply inside himself that he feared the flood of memories her words on the postcard might unleash. He was afraid of wanting her again and all that it would mean. Finally, he read her postcard. He read it three times. He remembered how it had been.

Chapter 1

When the conditions of a system in equilibrium are altered,
the equilibrium will shift in such a way as to attempt
to restore the initial condition.

LE CHÂTELIER'S PRINCIPLE

When he first saw her, the surf was battering the wide beach in advance of a spring storm, pounding like the thoughts that had urged him thousands of miles already. The cool air was layered with pockets of warmth, as though the Gulf Stream were washing up from the peninsula of Florida and lashing against a northeasterly cold front. The storm had taken his route, in a sense, shadowing his journey, weaving upcountry with him to the rough coast of Maine. He had hit the shore here like a ship on a reef. The engine in his van had finally quit dieseling, and he was off to pace the mile or two of beach that lay at the end of the state road. There was no more road left to drive.

The gray sea spit foam into the sky, as he let his feet sink into the damp sand. It sucked at him like wet concrete. How he wished it would swallow him whole. No one would ever find the body, and finally the town would tow away the old van, never knowing it had been nicknamed the Quark. Someone would toss out the junkyard of photos in back that meant nothing to anyone but him. He was alone now, a name that no one knew, a face that no one recognized. Only his driver's license betrayed who he had once been: Jackson Tate.

Lobster boats hurried back through the broad channel leading into the shelter of the harbor at Rockpoint. There was the sour brine of fish in the air. He heard the blast of an air horn from one of the small boats as it passed under the drawbridge that spanned the harbor. The pleasure boats, charter fishing rigs, and the high-mast sail boats were still in hibernation under blue shrink-wrap, waiting for the summer crowds to sail again. But the lobstermen had to pay the bills all year. They worked lashed by the spray of the Atlantic.

She was walking toward him bundled in burgundy-colored fleece. Her bronze hair was whipped by the wind, blown like petals around her face. She was the only splash of color in the bone gray of the shore, and later he would think that he was like an infant in that instant, his eyes just beginning to see in something more than black and white, beginning to see in primary colors. Anyway, he was drawn to her, as a child reaches for the first flower he sees as being yellow. And he was surprised by this stirring toward her, surprised as if by seeing yellow for the first time.

Like Jackson, she appeared to be isolated in her thoughts. "Excuse me," she said, as she looked up and saw that she had swerved into space that seemed private. She hadn't meant to come so close in all that vastness. Her eyes were green, the green of deep water. And even as he watched, a bright pinkness crept toward her face. She touched her neck as if to stop it. "I wasn't watching where I was going."

Jackson brushed the sweep of his gaze along the flat horizon, and thought that he liked her voice. It was musical, soothing as the sound of Irish. "It's easy to lose yourself here," he said.

"If only," she said, and laughed, vying with the wind, trying to keep the hair out of her eyes. It had copper strands, he could see now, that bright hair. It seemed to hold the only light in the dusk of the day. "If only."

He nodded. If only.

And then they parted.

Jackson hiked to the long jumble of rocks that formed a jetty on one side of the harbor entrance. He climbed out to the tip, balancing on the huge black boulders until there was nothing between him and the sea. The rocks were studded with barnacles and the tiny purple shells of periwinkles. The movement of the sea made an underwater grove of wide green seaweed sway like trees in the wind. Caught in the cracks between the rocks were dead crabs, picked apart by the seagulls that screamed with murderous delight as they swooped in on their prey.

Murder. There was that word again, creeping into his thoughts so innocently. He sucked in a deep draft of the ocean air. He could taste it on his tongue like tears. Simple salt—sodium chloride, meant to hydrate the blood and saturate the tissues, essential to life, yet we're only aware of this bitter saline when it flows from us. Jackson had not cried since it happened, and now he felt pent up in a way that even made it hard to swallow. No tears came anymore, just an echoing hollowness, like the massive empty bell of a nuclear reactor's containment building.

He was on his way back to the Quark when the sky began to turn from buttermilk to ash. In another time, he would have wanted to paint the scene, with the sky meeting the sea at the horizon and the stretch of beach. He would have even added the spot of burgundy that had been the woman's coat, the penny sheen of her hair. But he hadn't wanted to paint or work a stub of charcoal across his sketchbook in a long time now.

Parked at the curb was his van, which had carried him all this way: a well-used, burnt-sienna color, customized Econoline van that shimmied badly when he edged past sixty. Jackson didn't mind. After all, there was no place he had to be in a hurry. He had bought it from a dealer two hundred miles south of Wendell,

Illinois, south of home. The dealer had read about Jackson in the paper and knocked a couple of hundred bucks off the price.

It was a perfect setup, the Quark. After driving a while, Jackson could pull into a rest stop, turn off the engine, draw the green curtains on the windows in back, flip open the bunk, and sleep for a few hours. There was a gas stove that could boil water for soup or instant oatmeal in the morning. There was a foldout table where he could rest his head in his hands and think only of atoms spinning through space. Before long, always, the memories would return, and he would have to drive on, choosing back roads over the numbing rhythm of the interstate.

Back roads forced him to concentrate on his driving and gave him snapshot glimpses of picturesque towns, the comforting illusion of other people's calm lives. He didn't mind at all even if he was stuck behind a farmer in his tractor or an Amish family in their horse and buggy. The old highway system ran like veins over the landscape. Built before highway engineers dared to blast six lanes of straight asphalt across the earth, the older routes felt flexible enough to him to take their time to jog left or right or curl uphill around impediments. Those dual-lane highways were the way that everyone used to travel: lifeblood to distant hamlets, links between county seats. He liked to imagine, as he drove, how familiar this stretch of pavement was to someone, this oak-shaded curve, that peeling sign for Fanta root beer, the Phillips 66 station with one aging pump still squirting gas into rusty pickups. He was a stranger to these places where waitresses at the cafés called you by name, but there were those who knew this world as well as the rows in their hay fields. Even as he was consoled by the thought of the familiarity these roads held for its locals, he appreciated his own newness to them—their unexpected stoplights and hairpin curves and poorly marked intersections. Such conditions demanded more of a driver, and that fit Jackson's needs perfectly.

As he came off the beach and stepped over the curb in front of the Quark, he discovered a slick green pool of engine coolant. Opening the hood, he saw a bulbous, cracked radiator hose dribbling fluid through a split in its side. Another man might have spat out a curse and kicked the bumper, but Jackson had known what it was like to curse at the heavens for true tragedy, and he just shook his head. The Quark had brought him this far on only Jiffy-Lube oil changes and a brake job at a service station deep in New Jersey suburbia. He closed the hood and stomped around in a patch of grass to wick the slick coolant off his sneakers before he climbed inside.

The first fat drops of rain peppered the metal roof of the Quark as soon as he closed the door. He would have to wait until morning to walk the mile or so into town to find a replacement hose and a few gallons of coolant. It was getting dark, and he decided to spend the night where he was.

Jackson selected a can of tomato rice soup from his collection. He had a full shelf of red-and-white Campbell's cans—minestrone to Manhattan clam chowder—all secured by an elastic cord. He poured the soup into a blue speckled enameled pot on the gas burner and added a can of water from a plastic jug. In the cabinet that served as his pantry, he found a loaf of whole-grain bread he had bought at a bakery in a New Hampshire town. It was studded with enough oats and seeds to sow a half acre. On a low shelf against the floor were three thick photo albums he hadn't looked at since he'd left home. There was a toolbox filled with paints and bits of charcoal and several sketchbooks. Open on the floor was a paperback copy of *Ideas and Opinions*, by Albert Einstein, thumbed over like a family Bible. He picked up the book to read while his soup heated, but there was a sharp tap that seemed to stand out from the rain.

Jackson turned and in the rain-splattered twilight all he saw was his own reflection in the glass. His face was thin and ruggedly hewn, made more so by the brace of the salt air. He had unusually large dark brown eyes that had once looked on the world with far too much trust. There was a tiny arc of a scar on his well-defined chin. His hair was thick and rowdy with curls.

His eyes refocused as the sound repeated, and a sizzle of adrenaline jumped his heart when he saw the patrolman who rapped lightly on the window with the hard rubber end of a flashlight. The blood in Jackson's veins congealed and he had to force himself to take a breath. If it was going to end right there, with handcuffs biting into his wrists and the glassy eyes of camera lenses thrust up to his face, so be it. He had accepted fate's blows before and if he was out of road and out of time, he wouldn't fight it. In the moment that he took to move up front to the driver's seat and roll down the window, he decided not to run anymore.

"Sir," the officer said. His face was that of a teenager, with a smile that was a volatile mixture of perfunctory kindness and quiet disdain. A blemish flared on his cheek like Mount Vesuvius. "There's no overnight camping permitted here. I'll have to ask you to move along."

Jackson nodded, as he waited for a flicker of recognition to cross over the officer's eyes. His stomach quivered and he slowly turned his head forward to allow the officer to see his profile. Hadn't there been wanted posters printed with Jackson's picture in unfocused black and white at the top center, the nearly imperceptible scar on his chin listed under distinguishing marks? There had been no mug shots of course, but the newspaper had certainly taken enough pictures during those few days when his world collapsed that the police could have found one. Or they could have a grainy shot taken from the local TV news after they pounced on the story during a slow summer news day. Surely, he imagined, an all points bulletin had been issued to sheriff's offices cross-country by now? Or maybe the FBI had faxed his sheet from Washington out to all their regional offices? He had been dogged by worry his whole trip, obeying every posted speed limit just so he wouldn't run any risk of being pulled over. Maybe it just didn't matter anymore.

The patrolman's throat bobbed, and he continued, "There's a campground outside of town on Route 18."

"Sure, I'll find it," Jackson said, slowly concluding that he wasn't about to be thrown over the hood of the police car and frisked. And then he remembered. "But I can't move my vehicle. Busted radiator hose."

"Well," he said. "You'll have to find another place to spend the night. As for your vehicle, I can radio for a tow truck."

"That's not necessary, I'll take care of it."

"Yes sir, if that's what you want to do, then," the officer said with a quick nod of his head that knocked his visored hat down over his brow. He edged the hat back coolly, wished Jackson a good night, and returned to his car. Jackson cranked up the window. He looked around. Surely after the cop went on dinner break for a burger and chocolate shake he would circle back to check that he was gone. The town of Rockpoint had the quaint order of old-money resorts that probably didn't tolerate drifters like Jackson. He should have known better than to think he wouldn't stand out from the neatly shuttered summer cottages.

The simmer of his pot of soup called to him with a steady roil, and he went back to turn off the low blue flame. He stirred the soup with a metal spoon and lifted the blue enameled pot off the burner. Jackson hated to wash a dish if he didn't have to, and since he was alone, he ate directly from the saucepan. The soup warmed him in the tin can of his truck. On his journey, he had toured the temperate Gulf states first, then looped through Florida in the worst of the winter months, and then scooted up the East Coast into Maine. Even when he was trying to meander he made good time. His arrival was off, though, since he had landed far north, in the midst of a cool spring. Coming through Washington, the last of the cherry blossoms had been nipped by a cold snap and it was not the explosion of exuberant spring that he had expected.

There was an overnight bag in the storage bin under his bunk, and he packed it with a few essentials. Let them tow his truck to the police impound lot or cram citations under the wipers. He was finished with caring about those little things. The Quark wasn't going anywhere until he could get around to fixing it himself. And if the cop traced his license number and discovered who he was, what could he do? He locked the Quark, and took off on foot through a steady rain toward the light of a small inn he saw in the distance. The surf tumbled onto the beach at his back. He dodged puddles on the road as he hurried toward the wide curving porch of the house on the hilly rise of a protruding rocky neck of land. There were little gingerbread Victorian curlicues under the eaves. The cedar shakes illuminated by the porch light were bleached a light gray. The rain began to come down more urgently and Jackson hurried up the porch steps until he was under the roof. He rang the bell once to announce himself and stepped into the warmth of the lobby.

There was a slow fire glowing in the great stone fireplace. The polished wood floors were draped with thick Persian rugs. A huge curved wall of windows displayed the dark expanse of sea outside. There were comfortable chairs for reading or playing a rainy summer day backgammon game. A pair of French doors were open at one end, leading to a bar and small restaurant area. The lobby desk was an oak counter with a dozen room keys pigeonholed on the wall behind. On the desk was a brass hotel bell. Jackson held his hand over it and was about to ring when he saw her coming down the great curved staircase.

"I'm sorry, we're not open for the season yet," she said, before she recognized him. It was the woman from the beach. "Oh, hello. We've been running into each other all day."

"My truck broke down," Jackson said. "I was just passing through, but now I guess I'm looking for a place to stay."

"We're not really ready," she said, then seemed to hesitate inwardly. "But, I suppose I can make an exception. I always keep a few rooms made up." She moved behind the desk and opened the registration book. She hadn't met his eye. "I'll need your name and address right here."

"Thank you." He took the pen she handed him. "I didn't mean to wander in like this." He swept a hand through his hair and then wrote his name in her book. He had tried to avoid hotels on his journey, instead stopping in truck stops to buy a shower or pay a few dollars to park overnight in a campground. The dark rooms of roadside hotels made him feel too isolated, and though he had money, he didn't know how long he would need to make it last.

He wrote down his address in Illinois as she ran his credit card through, and just printing the words called up the image of that old farmhouse in the midwestern university town, where he had lived with his family. The house stood at the eastern edge of the corn belt that stretched across the midriff of Missouri and Kansas, to touch the Colorado border. There were old photographs at the Wendell historical museum of men in dust-mottled suits and their families in their best clothes from the Sears catalog at a family gathering on what later became Jackson's front porch. By then, the cornfields were planted over with grassy lawns and the family farm was only an acre-sized patch of land surrounded by suburban ranches hedged with newly planted oaks stunted by the wind. Jackson's home seemed on higher ground because of the lofty tree-tops of the mature shade trees. There was also a pond out back and a sour cherry tree that yielded enough for a half dozen pies every spring.

He stopped himself.

"Welcome, Mr. Tate," the woman said when Jackson turned the registration card toward her. She brought her eyes up to his, then looked away before saying, "I'm Olivia Faraday, but my friends call me Livvy."

"Glad to meet you, Livvy," he said. "And call me Jackson, please. Only my students use Tate."

"I can do that." She smiled enough for him to see the white gleam of her teeth. She glanced at his address. "Wendell, Illinois. I used to live in Chicago."

"Really?" Jackson said. He allowed himself to see how beautiful she was: The hair had been tamed to a sheen now and caught back in a ponytail that brushed the collar of her sweater. Her eyes were darker by lamplight, sad. They gave her an age belied by her bud of a nose and some slight freckles on her cheeks. She had to be about his age, he thought, still in her thirties.

"Do you teach at the university there?"

"Stayed on after I got my Ph.D."

"So tonight, we really will have a doctor in the house," she said with a quick laugh, then she blushed suddenly as she had on the beach when they had encountered each other, when she had been embarrassed at finding herself face to face with him. Now, her own laughter seemed to have startled her, to have thrown her off balance, and she struggled to regain herself. Her awkwardness touched him, even as she turned her attention to choosing a room for him.

"You'll want an ocean view. Everyone does," she said. "Let me put you in number three. I think that's made up. Anyway, that's the best of them." She took the key from its place. All business now.

"Must be quiet this time of year," he said, following her upstairs. He liked that voice, the soft lilting quality of it, the music. He didn't want her to stop talking to him.

"Dead is more like it, but it'll start picking up soon."

"You ever think of closing the place up in the winter and heading to Florida?"

"My husband and I used to travel every year," she said. "Europe or the Caribbean, depending on our mood. But we don't go anywhere now."

"I've never been to Europe," he said. "Although, I did spend three fascinating months conducting research at an observatory on a rat-infested island in the South Pacific."

"You'd love Europe," she said passionately, then catching herself, added: "I can't imagine anyone not loving it, I mean. The food, the art. I miss it." She stopped, tossed off another of her quick self-conscious laughs. "Good grief, we can't have everything, right?"

"Sounds like the chasm principle at work," Jackson said.

"The chasm principle?"

"Just one of my theories."

"Like Einstein's?" she teased, letting her eyes skitter toward his, then away.

He laughed, bayed almost, and felt immediately how out of scale it was to her little jab. It had just been a long time, hadn't it? He wrenched himself into a grin and explained: "Not that caliber of theory, not hardly, just something I concocted about the tremendous, earth-swallowing gap between the life you want and the life you're leading at that moment. For some reason that gap, or chasm, or Grand Canyon, is directly proportional to how much you want."

"The larger the desire, the greater the chasm," she said, nodding. "Always seems that way. And you are professor of . . . ?"

"Physics," Jackson said. "Alfred W. Blauman Professor of Physics." He suddenly felt embarrassed and pretentious at so glibly announcing his official title, and backpedaled. "The department chair didn't have any other nominees the year my name came up."

"The chasm principle," she repeated. "I like that."

He followed her along the wide, thickly carpeted hallway. She opened the door to his room for him and flicked on the lamp on the bedside table. She ran a hand across the bedspread to smooth a ripple of fabric, seeming suddenly nervous again, as though she had never mustered the nerve to joke with him, to laugh. "Can I get you anything?" she asked. There was a brusqueness about her, a retreat into professional hospitality. "A drink or a sandwich from the kitchen?"

"Nope, I'm fine," he said, not because he wasn't hungry (he was ravenous) but because he couldn't torture her anymore with his presence. The red flush that crept up her throat and into her face looked hot and uncomfortable as a rash. Best to keep his distance. Either she feared him: Where was her husband anyway? Was he somewhere in the house, or was Livvy alone and unnerved by having a male guest? But then why hadn't she just relied on the truth, which was that the inn was closed for the season? Had she needed the price of the room that badly? Or maybe, probably, it was only that she was shy, maybe innkeeping abraded her personality. Maybe her husband was more of an innkeeper. In any case, Jackson would leave her to herself. He had packed some crackers in his bag.

"Well, then, breakfast is at eight," she said.

"Thanks again for letting me stay."

She nodded, then crossed the room and rested a hand on the doorknob. "Good night," she said. She tried to look at him, but couldn't pull it off. She swung the door closed behind her.

And he was alone again.

Chapter 2

*Every body continues in its state of rest, or of uniform motion
in a right line, unless it is compelled to change that
state by forces impressed upon it.*

NEWTON'S FIRST LAW OF MOTION

In the morning, Jackson stretched back on the queen-sized bed,
where he lay under a quilt. It was a patchwork of colored bands
that made him think of the rings of Saturn. He touched its stitches
with his fingertips and watched the sun rise from the dead black
sea. The light glowed and pulsed through the wavy antique glass
panes of the leaded windows, filling the room and casting the sea
a brilliant cobalt. For the first time since he was forced to sleep

without her, he had slept through the night. His mind hadn't churned like a machine, forcing him to drift in and out of dreams that were every bit as horrifying as his waking hours. His thoughts over the last months had been layered into a Möbius strip, trapping him in a dizzying loop of that last day and those murky weeks afterward.

Mornings would never be the same for Jackson. He ground through the empty predawn, when every hope that buoyed him through the day was extinguished by the suffocating darkness. By morning, hope would return, crippled and staggering toward him, allowing him to draw a single breath and believe for an instant that life was as it had always been: His son and daughter, kneading the sleep from their eyes. Nancy's soft breath tickling his ear as she spooned him. On weekends, the two of them would lie in bed late and listen to the children. Fire and brimstone trailed up from the TV, in front of which Nathan was parked, inexplicably choosing the Hieronymus Bosch descriptions of hellfire and damnation by a cable station evangelist over the Cartoon Network. He shushed his little sister, Franny, who was busy inventing the fifteenth verse of "I'm a Little Teapot."

Only when Jackson's full waking consciousness intruded did the buzz of their lives in his head scatter like the billion-year-old dust drifting through the solar system. And he felt paralyzed again.

After they were gone, he broke things. His things, not theirs. The clock-radio by the bedside, his sunglasses, and even his treasured fly-fishing rod were all kindling for his fury. One evening, haunted and bitter, he kicked over the telescope on the front porch, where some weeks before they had all taken turns watching the red dot of Mars when its elliptical orbit had drawn close to Earth's. When the telescope broke, the glass lenses inside it shattered with a quiet pop, and when he picked up the metal tube, the fragments of glass tumbled out with a sound like rain. He was a stranger to this violence that seemed to surge forth from somewhere inside him like the fiery explosions he had seen emanating from the surface of the sun.

As time passed, his grief shook everything out of him until he dissolved like a chunk of rock salt on a wet road. It made him feel as if he were living outside himself, witnessing his own passage into another realm of time and space. He felt as though he were becoming two-dimensional, flattening into a broad ribbon of flesh. His grief grabbed hold of him at the most unexpected places: Pushing a cart down the aisle at a supermarket, he would suddenly become aware of something—the kids' Cocoa Puffs, his wife's herbal shampoo. His grief would whirl through him like a tornado. Pushing his cart toward the cash registers, his face twisted by the agonizing sadness in his head, he would hear people whisper, and some would offer sympathy. They knew his face from the newspapers and the Channel 12 cameras jammed in front of him, closing in for a poignant, teary breakdown. He didn't seem to have the emotional strength to hold himself together. And eventually, he crumbled.

It had happened during the summer break at the university,

while Jackson's colleagues were teaching summer school for extra cash or locked in basement labs experimenting in the darkness. Jackson himself had spent three weeks that June conducting research in particle physics at an institute in California. Fourteen hours a day he accelerated protons through a long circular tube pulsating with a magnetic field. It was a study of matter-antimatter collisions. Antimatter behaves just like ordinary matter, but a violent result occurs should they be mixed. Collisions are marked by a burst of gamma radiation. All day, Jackson shot a shower of quarks at antiquarks and used a specially coated photographic plate to record the results, letting the blip of a gamma ray reveal the tragic meeting of charged particles. The energy released is equal to mc^2 (where m is mass and c is the speed of light), or, as expressed in Einstein's simple equation, $E = mc^2$. Einstein theorized that as a particle's velocity increased toward the speed of light, its mass would increase as well, and therefore a continually greater amount of energy would be needed to propel it. It reminded Jackson of a dream that used to recur, before all his dreams were blotted away, of swimming languidly in blue tropical waters suddenly pierced by shark fins. In his dream he tried to swim, but instead got nowhere at all.

Jackson had returned from his trip to California with new research for a paper he planned to write, but he was in no mood to work. His young children were done with their school year and his wife was on vacation. He loved the summer at home with his family, taking them to swim in the pool on campus or pulling weeds with them in the vegetable garden. There wasn't as much time as he had thought there would be, though it was the longest summer of his life.

By September everything had changed. The life had bled instantly out of the farmhouse they had carefully decorated with country antiques. Jackson himself was empty of life as he sat alone at the long pine kitchen table unshaven, staring into the oily void of a cup of coffee. He left the lights burning through the day and night until the wiring of the antique floor lamp in the den, where he had read *Dr. De Soto* to Franny just one more time before bed, crackled and fizzled in a puff of electrical pique.

There was no reason, it seemed to him, only a blind will that moved unwaveringly forward. The arrow of time sliced through the thick muscle of his heart. Memory exposes like film, and we're free to toy with past time, run it forward and backward, pausing, zooming, and viewing our history in slow motion like movie directors. The present yields to the past as soon as thought captures it, sinking flitting moments into the golden amber of memory. The future runs head-on into us like the sharks of Jackson's dreams, fast, unpredictable, and with razored fangs slashing.

Afterward, he often thought of Newton's Third Law of Motion: For every action there is an equal and opposite reaction. That law ruled everything in the universe, from the tug of the earth's gravity to the planets strung out like beads off the sun. And it ruled him now. He was his own lesson in particle acceleration. He had to keep moving.

He escaped with what was most dear to him—the photographs of their life as a family. His wife, Nancy, was the family photojournalist, snapping at birthdays, picnics, and meandering Sunday afternoons when they'd barbecue and squeeze homemade lemonade. On days like that, time moved in jerky fits and starts. An hour lasted forever, but when the end of the day drew close, time had slipped away like sand. Thinking of how he had held her hand tightly, laced up his fingers with hers, was the only way he could calm himself now.

When he had finally left the house, and had run out on his job, he was desperate. The memories lived within him. His family was more than the tapestry-covered couch, Nathan's Batman sheets, or the goldfish swimming in the backyard pond. They were the essence of how they had lived and loved one another. Jackson thought that was the mistake people made in judging him. It was too intense for him to go on surrounded by their echoes. And after all that he'd done, he had to escape. What he did was pure survival instinct to preserve what was left of his annihilated heart.

After all, no one could really have expected him to live closed up in that house, wandering from bedroom to bedroom through the horrible night, reliving their lives in his memory. Those evenings had passed in silence, his fork stabbed into some reheated casserole or stew that had been stacked in the freezer by competing Good Samaritan friends. Jackson could only hear their concern as a white-noise buzz. He thanked the neighbors, the mothers of Franny's preschool friends, and his university colleagues, but they were outside of what he felt. How could he share his feelings when he was caught up, alone, in solitary.

To him, time didn't seem to be moving forward at all. The days after he had lost them, he had been in no condition to plan another year of lessons in quantum mechanics or Newtonian physics. He couldn't continue to teach about the unyielding laws that governed the universe, not when his life had been so shattered by its randomness. Physics explained the mechanics of the tragedy, but nothing explained the act itself, the terrible result. Jackson knew that he couldn't stand in front of a lecture hall filled with a hundred students and explain Newton's Laws of Motion because he knew too well how they had been applied to his own family. He had witnessed the effects of acceleration in the direction of the applied force. And the way that bodies of unequal weight will fall through space at the same rate. He knew exactly what those bodies looked like when they had impacted a fixed position. He knew their faces, their names, their ages. He knew that his wife, Nancy, loved to take Nathan and Franny shopping for clothes. And when they got home, she'd call for a "fashion show" and the kids would try on their new outfits and parade through the upstairs bedrooms. It was a moment of unbridled vanity, but they couldn't resist showing off for their dad, who had been closeted in his lab at the university. The colors of their new denims and Franny's white blouses were almost brighter than his eyes could stand. They bounced, preened, and howled with energy that both delighted and exhausted him, and he would wonder for a moment if his wife had given birth to two brilliant quarks instead.

Once he came home to find them in the backyard, swinging in the hammock with a book. Nancy was holding Franny in her lap, while the girl squirmed, reaching out to yank on her brother's golden blond hair. To her his hair must have looked like a brilliant corona framing his head. Jackson stood on the cool grass watching the three of them. They hadn't heard him pull up. Nancy was listening to Nathan stumble through a passage, sounding out the words slowly, correcting himself when he was wrong, and she'd stroke Franny when she got restless. In that moment, still standing there, Jackson knew it was a snapshot he would always recall. He did over and over again, and now the pain was so palpable he could feel it clench his throat and burn his eyes.

Jackson moved stiffly from his bed at the Rockpoint Inn. His body was so used to sleeping on the hard plank in the Quark that it almost didn't know how to relax into the comfort of a fine mattress. That was something he could get used to again, he supposed. He washed and dressed quickly, choosing clean clothes from his bag. Over the last months, he had become quite adept at finding laundromats and doing the wash. Feeding the quarters into the machines reminded him of his college days, when he did the laundry only at the point where the ripeness of his clothes offended him. But that was years ago, before Nancy looked out for him.

Jackson found himself thinking of Livvy as he left his room, of her gentleness and good humor, of the way her awareness of him showed in the flush of her skin, the quickness of her laugh. This he had sorely missed over the last year, this sensation of seeing himself in someone else's reaction: interaction. If there was one thing that Jackson had learned in his travels, it was that too often it seemed that kindness had been drained from people like old crankcase oil. When some waitress or a gas station attendant smiled and made small talk for a few minutes, it meant something to him. It cracked through his isolation. But it happened so infrequently. And in terms of sheer meanness, the other drivers on the road were the worst. They'd cut you off and wave a fist at you just for breathing the same air. Of course, Jackson in the Quark, with the center of gravity as high as Everest, was a prime target for road rage. Driving those winding secondary roads was a challenge at rapid speed, and Jackson would always have some yahoo in a late-model muscle car or a pumped-up pickup truck riding his tail until he could pull over and let them pass.

From the top of the stairs, he could smell the coffee and the muffins, and the lovely scent drew him down into the sunny lobby and through the French doors into the small back dining room with a half dozen tiny square tables. There was only one table set, with smooth stoneware plates and a heavy mug. A fresh-cut daffodil stood in a tiny crystal vase on the center of the table. Jackson sat down and read the note perched on the napkin. He examined the fine blond writing paper that had flower petals pressed into its fibers. He ran his fingers over a gauzy violet petal and next to it, a fleck of marigold. The message was for him and he read the fine even strokes of the fountain pen.

Dear Jackson,

Please forgive me. I've been called away this morning. Enjoy the blueberry muffins (my specialty). There's plenty of coffee brewed (it's French roast). Have as many refills as you'd like.

Livvy Faraday

A sensation bloomed in him, and he recognized it as disappointment. He had missed her by minutes. Time for the rest of the world seemed to continue, but for Jackson it would always seem frozen in his most horrible moments. He tucked Livvy's note away in his shirt pocket and pulled the napkin off the basket, revealing two muffins the size of softballs. He poured himself a cup of coffee from the glass carafe and set it back on the warmer. The muffins exploded with berries when he split one apart, and it was warm and tangy with lemon and sour cream. They were the best he'd ever had.

Nancy had never indulged much in breakfast, but it was Jackson's favorite meal of the day. He and Nathan would slip out in the cool early morning and eat at a diner with chipped Formica tabletops and reconstituted orange juice. But it was the pancakes they came for. There were at least a dozen varieties and Jackson hoped to try them all. He mostly stuck with the whole grain and bran variety while he encouraged Nathan to have something fun. If Nathan had a short stack of chocolate chip pancakes, Jackson knew he could sneak a few bites from the boy's plate. That was enough for him. It broke Nancy's rules about too much sugar for breakfast, but he could see how happy it made his son.

Breakfast out was a Sunday-morning tradition that he had started with his own father. Jackson remembered going out early to Joe's, a lunch counter in the New York City suburbs with a soda fountain and booths upholstered in brown vinyl. They'd sit over plates of fried eggs, sopping up runny yolk with toast. Jackson's father would sip black coffee and flip through the newspaper he had bought up front at the cash register. Or if they had stayed home for a cold breakfast, they would motor over in the white Chrysler sometime in the afternoon for the paper and Jackson could sit at the counter and sip a chocolate milk shake through a thick wax paper straw. His father might even buy him a Superman comic book for a quarter. Jackson felt that those little rituals were important to a father and son. Maybe it fulfilled a primitive hunter-gatherer instinct. Instead of hunting down a wild antelope together, a father taught his son to stalk and snare a five-pound Sunday *New York Times* and carry it back for the family. Arts and Leisure, Sports, and Business were what man needed to get ahead in the world.

Jackson had wondered recently, during his most alone hours, what his father would have thought about what he had done. His father was a tax accountant who followed the rules so stridently that he died nearly to the day his insurance actuary chart determined he would, allowing for the standard deductions for a cigar smoker with high blood pressure and a heart murmur. He never officially retired from the oil company he worked for that was run by a Texan who liked to break in a new pair of snakeskin boots by striding up and down the sidewalk outside headquarters on Lexington Avenue, dictating to a secretary. Jackson's father was a former navy man with a closetful of white shirts starched and pressed into right angles by the Chinese-owned laundry in town. Before bed, he did thirty push-ups, just like he had done during his three-year stint. Jackson witnessed these ablutions and he found their order strangely comforting. His father had a wooden shoeshine kit with polish and brushes under the lid, and Sunday evenings he would place a wing tip on the kit's stand and put a shine on it. After he was gone, people recalled him as a shy man. But his mother said wistfully that he was a navy man through and through.

"You have to stand up for yourself," his father had once told Jackson in a dark moment when his bitterness surfaced. "Nobody's going to do it for you."

His name had been David, Jackson's father, and he had organized the world between the straight blue lines that marked the ledgers where he kept track of the household finances. There was a code David Tate followed, as ancient as Hammurabi's Babylonian rules, engraved in the granite tablet of Jackson's memory. It was a code that was evident in the addition and subtraction by number two Eberhard Faber yellow pencils and colored pens that David lined up on his desk as though he were arranging arrows for battle. A Pink Pearl eraser stood by like a medic to stanch the rare miscalculation. At intervals determined by a fiscal calendar of his own devising, David set into a pile of grocery-store receipts that his mother dug from the dark recesses of her purse. She saved every scrap of paper for him to tally the numbers. She was afraid not to.

David worked the numbers on a Burroughs adding machine with a total-key that stuck. It spit out a paper tape with all the answers, and Dave wrote them down in the ledger book. Income was inked in black; expenses were entered in red. By the end of the year, everything would be in place for income tax forms. He could fill them out in an afternoon every January second. And the code was simple: The numbers always had to come out in the black. It was in the red where disaster could happen. Splayed on the carpet next to his father's desk, calculating his own sums from the problems in his school math book, Jackson listened to his father warn of the doom of foreclosure, repossession, and bankruptcy. Those were the terrible things that could happen should one make the mistake of sliding into the delinquency of red.

Maybe Jackson hoped to prove something when he began making calculations in the predictable chaos of the world of physics. He found an easy familiarity to problem solving and had an aptitude for numbers that reached into the powers of ten. There was safety in numbers. Jackson's view of the world was filtered through the red digits lined up on the screen of his Texas Instruments scientific calculator. It kept life at a distance.

Nancy always let him be. Jackson was her mad scientist, and while she could thread her arms around the kids all day, he held back. Some deep place inside him was frightened of the way that love and family reveal the soul inside.

"That's who you are, Jackson," she had told him once after an argument. "I realized years ago that you're like one of those people who can't stand bright light. That happens to you emotionally, Jackson. You can't stand the brightness of your own feelings. I know you love us, but you filter it through your work, to look at us all from a safe distance." She was right. Jackson couldn't help himself. He felt stricken. "Don't look so shocked," she said. "One day, I'll get you to crack."

In a sense, she finally did.

After his solitary breakfast at the inn, Jackson cleared the table and did the dishes in the galley kitchen behind a double-hinged door. In a kitchen drawer he found a roll of foil, and he wrapped the second muffin. It would make a good snack at some point in the day. He switched off the coffee brewer and went into the lobby to find a phone book. He wasn't going anywhere until he fixed that blown hose on the Quark. There was an auto parts store in town, and he called for directions.

The thick front lawn of the inn was terraced with flower beds and short paths dusted with finely crushed pink granite. The early-spring flowers of narcissus and grape hyacinths poked their heads up, their veiny translucent blooms shimmering in the cool morning light. Jackson headed down the main path that was edged carefully with cobblestone. There was a simple bench made of weathered planks, which was tucked between two white cedars that had been meticulously shaped. Someone had carved a small heart into one of the rough cedar planks of the seat.

Thirty minutes later, having found the parts he needed, Jackson returned to the Quark. When he had passed it on his way into town, he had found no tickets piled under the wipers and the beast hadn't been towed. He threw open the hood and began poking through his tool kit for the right size screwdriver. He pushed up his sleeves, then removed the clamps holding the remains of the bulging rubber radiator hose and pulled the thing off. A dribble of coolant ran from the hose, and he wrapped it in a few sheets of newspaper. He slipped the replacement hose on the radiator and connected it tightly, before refilling the coolant reservoir. As he was putting away his tools and wiping the grease off his hands with a soft rag, he happened to glance at the Winnie-the-Pooh cartoon figures on the fabric. It was a square cut from one of Nathan's old flannel pajamas. Jackson gripped the fabric in his fist. It had been in his tool kit for some time, mundane, a rag: until now.

He was distracted by the sound of a car slowing, and Livvy

pulled up beside him driving a silver Volvo station wagon. He folded the rag into a neat square and laid it inside his tool kit.

"Good morning," she said, as she rolled down her window. "How's the car?"

"Nothing major," he said. "Just a radiator hose."

"Did you find your breakfast all right?" The sun was shining in her face, and she shielded her eyes with the flat of a hand. It seemed to shield her from him too and made her seem more sure of herself today, less unhinged by his presence.

"I might want your recipe for those muffins," he said.

She laughed. "I'd lose a lot of repeat customers if I gave them a recipe—instead of a reason to come back."

Now he laughed. "Ah, I see, you're a calculating business-woman."

"Usually," she said. "Sorry I had to leave you on your own this morning. I'm usually a better host than that." She shifted the car into park, seemed to collect herself again, got serious. "There's a great mechanic in town if you need him. He kept my husband's old Fiat going years after it should have been scrapped."

"Thanks, but it's all done." Jackson flicked a clot of dark grease out from under a fingernail. The husband again.

"So you're coming back to the inn?"

"I'll be there in a few minutes," he said. "To settle up."

She nodded and waved, then rolled up her window and drove slowly up the road. He latched his tool kit containing the scrap of Pooh pajamas. He slid it under the front passenger seat.

Jackson climbed in, turned the key, and the engine on the Quark coughed back to life, ready to go. The steady vibration rattled the loose vents on the dashboard. He revved it a bit to get the water pump circulating the new coolant. Afterward, he got out and watched the engine, scanning for leaks. It was all dry. Closing the hood, he put the car into drive and swung a U-turn. For the first time in months, he drove back along the way he had come.

Chapter 3

Force, as well as motion, is a relative quantity. Gravitation
can be interpreted as a distortion in space that
surrounds every mass in the universe.

EINSTEIN'S THEORY OF GENERAL RELATIVITY

Livvy had pulled the Volvo up to the kitchen door. Jackson parked
the van along the curb and saw that she was carrying in bags of
groceries, so he walked along the side driveway toward her. "Here,
let me get that for you," Jackson said, reaching for a plastic bag
that was beginning to split at the bottom seam.

"Thanks." She sighed. "It's been one of those mornings."

He could see that in her eyes. The intensity he had noticed in them the day before seemed to have shattered into distraction.

"Don't sweat it," he told her. "A chemist friend of mine has discovered a formula for increasing the tensile strength of these plastic bags ten times. If the patent clears, soon you'll be able to carry a bowling ball or two home from the supermarket."

"Or at least a quart of milk," she said. There was something in her voice that he recognized, a straining to make herself sound normal. He heard the effort.

He held the bag with one hand and propped the back door open for her with the other. She slipped under his arm and went inside.

"Here?" He gestured to the butcher-block table with the bag in his hand. She nodded, and he set the bag down.

She tucked an errant strand of hair behind her ear and put away the groceries in the pantry. Jackson slipped into the small restroom off the bar, where he washed away the smears of grease and dirt from his car repairs.

"I see you cleaned up after yourself," she said, gesturing to the dining room he had neatened after breakfast.

"Well, I felt like I should, being your only guest. Besides, I hate to leave behind a tableful of dirty dishes."

"Follow that advice and you could run the place," she said. "So, what brings you to the Maine coast?"

He shrugged. What could he say to make her understand? He tried to recall their brief conversation from last night when he had felt so bleary from exhaustion and hunger. "I've taken some time away this year. I'll get back to teaching one of these days."

"The guys in the physics department used to scare me when I was in college," she said. "All those men in black-rimmed plastic glasses."

"Please." He took mock offense. "My colleagues and I have been working hard for years to get anyone associated with physics into contact lenses. Forget subatomic particle research, that's been our greatest challenge."

She laughed and then self-consciously brought her fingers up to adjust the tiny silver bauble that had twisted on her earring. "I guess I judged them unfairly. But that world seems so impenetrable to me. Maybe because I never went very far in science."

"A lot of teachers bore kids with formulas and numbers," he said. "But if you reduce it to its basic elements, most people find it very straightforward. Logical, even." Jackson taught the physics of the everyday, like the balance struck between speed and centrifugal force that kept the Quark from leaving the road on a curve.

"It's hard to get over the feeling that science can solve anything," she said, softly. "I guess you grow to expect it." The strain again, the subterranean bulge under her tone of voice, threatening to crack through with what she felt compelled to hide. Her eyes studied something out the window.

"The white knight of science," Jackson agreed, although he wasn't sure whether she was listening or was instead lost, sunk down into what lay deep within her and kept swelling up into her eyes, her voice, her ears; choking her, blinding her, deafening her to everything close by, anything she might reach out and actually touch.

Still, Jackson kept talking, as much for himself as for her. He didn't want to break what small connection had been established, this flow of words between them. These last nine months, Jackson had been skittish of any relationship that endured longer than the time it took for a gas station attendant to make change for a twenty. He respected emotional distance like a lead-lined jar of plutonium. But for the first time since he had lost the ones he most wanted to be near, he found that he needed this, however fleeting it might be. He needed this. Something in her had reached that old place in him that yearned for company.

He said: "It took me a long time to realize that people aren't always clear where imagination ends and science begins. You wouldn't believe how many beginning students I have every year who want to build some kind of science fiction transporter beam that will shoot their molecules across the universe to be reassembled on the other side. And when I tell them the only people who can do that work for Paramount Studios in Hollywood, they're crushed. So I don't tell them that anymore. Instead, we've tried to prove the fiction using science."

"You mean with experiments?" she said. Her gaze had come indoors, and it shifted to his.

"Sure, experiments, theories, chemistry, biology, whatever we could throw at the problem." He was the one who looked away now. That green, those depths.

"And what did you come up with?"

"All kinds of crazy stuff," Jackson said. "But it was the best way to teach Einstein's theories. Although, mostly what I found was that some people really need the fantasy to pay attention to the big picture. There's a whole link between science and the imagination that's right out of the movies I saw and comic books I read when I was a kid. It isn't easy to forget that dreamy world of possibility."

She sighed, and their eyes caught on each other's again. The phone rang sharply and Jackson saw Livvy stiffen.

"I'm sorry," Jackson said. "I'm going on too much." He waved toward the phone, as if she needed his permission.

"No, not at all. Let me just get that."

He was hungry for this, for the nourishment that conversation provided. Nancy told him once that he was a reactive conversationalist—waiting for the right personality to mesh with his before he could converse easily. He always felt that he needed a catalyst to nudge him into a freewheeling mode, and it happened only rarely. He kept them close to him—a few friends, Nancy and the children—they stirred something in him that coupled the links in his train-of-thought. Otherwise, he too often let himself regress and held people at a distance with a recalcitrant, almost sullen demeanor. For whatever reason, Livvy was a catalyst and she could lure him out of his shyness. He waited for her to finish her call, flipping through a stack of brochures for whale-watch cruises and bike rentals, hoping that the call wouldn't go on so long that his feigned interest in local tourist attractions would start to look feigned.

"I told you last night that I was fine, George," he heard her say, trying to mask a mild irritation. "I don't want you coming out here and risking your health. It can wait until you're better. If it rains again I'll get a bucket brigade going. No, please, I'm kidding. You just relax and let Mary take care of you. Okay, George. Bye-bye."

"Trouble?" Jackson asked when she hung up. Immediately he was twinged by how inappropriate his question was. What business was it of his?

She didn't seem to notice. "Just an overprotective handyman," she said. "He fell off a ladder last week and broke his leg. He's got no business going up on ladders anyway since he's nearly eighty years old. But I have a leaky roof and he was worried about how it fared in the rain last night."

"How did it?"

"Not well. I was up all night emptying buckets."

"I would have helped," Jackson offered.

"No paying guest should ever have to pitch in. That's one of my house rules." She laughed and touched his arm with a light motion.

"Are you trying to remind me to pay my bill?"

She flushed. "No." Then she saw how he was grinning and regained her footing. "I have your credit card number, remember?"

"Ah, yes, of course." He laughed, then: "Let me take a look at that roof for you. Maybe there's something I can do."

It was an impulse. He didn't know if she could be persuaded, but he wanted to offer. He wanted to do something for this woman he hardly knew, who had already done something for him, even if it was just to send a tracery of sensation into areas of his psyche that had been numb for months now, atrophied.

Livvy seemed to him so fragile somehow, the way her life-blood rose into her cheeks, burned there. There was something so transparent about her, so diaphanous that her emotions showed on the surface. Maybe her sensitive skin was wrapped around a skeleton of hardened blue steel; he didn't know her well enough to know. It had been that way with his Nancy. She was always so resilient. Recalling her strength had helped him these last months. But Livvy, with a laugh she held too long and eyes bruised by sorrow, whatever strength she had seemed on the verge of crumbling. At least he could have a look at her leaky roof. If he couldn't touch that look in her eyes, patch up whatever sorrow she had, at least he could take care of what was made of wood and tar and tile. He could help with the house, this sprawling inn.

Nancy had always told Jackson that he was an expert at helping others, but was obstinate about helping himself. He'd leave the house in a T-shirt during winter, after making sure the kids were snuggled tight. And it was clear that when he cooked a meal, it was for others, since he could make do with a cold sandwich. Being married to Nancy had taught him some hard lessons about who he was in the world.

It wasn't all that difficult for Jackson to persuade Livvy to let him take a look at the leaky roof. She was a little embarrassed about it, but her relief was more in evidence. She relented quickly, and together they trudged up to the top floor where the ceiling was colored with yellow waterstains. There were several buckets still on the carpet.

"Really, it's such a mess up here," she said. "I shouldn't have bothered you."

"It's nothing," Jackson said. "At my farmhouse, there was always something like frozen pipes or a family of mice in the walls. You don't have mice, do you?"

"God, I hope not." She shuddered.

"Don't worry. I'm good with mice."

"I think I'd have to move if we had, you know . . ."

"Mice?"

Livvy cringed. "I can't bear to think of them, those beady eyes and little snouts in the air."

"Their claws scratching in the walls."

"Please," she shouted, covering her ears.

"Okay, okay," Jackson said, laughing. "Have you been up into the attic to look around?"

"No, I was saving that for George," she said. "I haven't been up there for a long time, might run into, you know . . . You're welcome to take a look, though."

Jackson pulled on the cord that hung down from the access panel in the ceiling. A folded stairway gently creaked open and Jackson locked it in position on the carpeted floor. He stepped up into the attic and pulled a chain, switching on a bare bulb. Livvy followed him up the stairs.

He stepped carefully in the attic, following the wooden planks that bridged the rafters. The water that had dripped through the roof had stained a trail as it followed the rafters and the joists. Jackson made a thorough inspection.

"It looks bad, but a leaky roof is never that serious," he said. "It's just a matter of patching holes."

"I know," she sighed. "But my maintenance fund is pretty tapped out this year. I thought George could rig up a temporary fix. You know, bubble gum or something." She grinned, tried to belie the seriousness of her plight.

"I don't know if an old man with his leg in a cast would be much good to you on a job like this."

"You're right, you're right." She shook her head as if she should have known better. "My husband would know what to do, but George sort of came with the house."

"Why don't you let me take a crack at it?"

"I couldn't. That's very kind of you, but I couldn't ask."

"You don't have to ask. I'm offering. I have time to spare, and summer construction work helped pay my way through college."

"I'd insist on paying you," she said.

"If you want me to give you a bloated estimate with built-in overtime, I can. I know exactly how to do it. Otherwise, just think of it as getting some help from a friend."

She shook her head.

"Give me room and board, then."

This made her smile. "Twist my arm." She looked him full in the eyes, didn't flinch away.

Which almost unnerved him. He said, "Can I keep the same room?"

"Sure," she said. "Or you can sleep in a different bed every night if you want. There are twelve to choose from."

"Then it's a deal."

Jackson offered his hand to close their negotiations. Livvy's tapered fingers were cool in his clasp, and he felt her polished nails brush against the tender skin of the inside of his wrist. It was the first touch he had received from a woman in months now.

The attic was a jumble of dismantled bed frames, old furniture, and mattresses that had mildewed under the leaking roof. It seemed typical for a hotel storage area. But near the stairway was a garment rack filled with dark pinstriped business suits on wooden hangers. There was a dresser with pairs of wing-tip shoes set neatly on top. Wooden shoe trees maintained their shapes so they'd be ready to slip on, but a thick coating of dust marred their shine. Jackson looked at the suits on the rack in the shadowy sunlight that streamed in through the far portals.

"They're my husband's," she said, when she noticed his gaze. She wiped the dust from her palms and then ran a hand over them. He noticed her face had clouded.

"I guess he doesn't have much reason to dress up for work in Rockpoint," he said.

"No, but he was always ready to get back into a courtroom."

"What made him decide to leave?"

"Oh, he didn't want to go, but you know how messy the corporate world can be. There are always casualties. Howard was something of an innocent bystander, I guess."

"I'm sorry to hear that," Jackson said. He worried that he was wading into waters that were too deep for people who hadn't known each other very long. But he suspected that Livvy would let him know when his curiosity got him in over his head.

"Howard is older than I am," she said. "He'll be sixty this year. He always thought it was funny about how he had just passed the bar exam the year I was born."

"It must take a lot of work for both of you to keep this place in shape," Jackson said. "The gardens alone look like a full-time job." He knew he was baiting her. But he wanted to know, and not about how the gardening and hosting duties were divvied up. He suddenly found himself wanting to know *with whom*, what kind of man. He cared to know.

"When we bought the inn five years ago," she said, "Howard loved fixing it up. He had spent summers here on the coast when he was growing up and I guess he wanted to return to the place where he had been happiest. We'd only been married a few years, but I was ready to leave Chicago for something different."

They climbed down the attic stairs and Jackson folded them back into the ceiling. She had fallen silent, her wide lips were seamed together and her eyes showed the pain again. He didn't press her toward anymore revelation, only said, "I should probably get started while the weather's good." He hoped it would shift the subject back to a less personal arena, was ashamed of himself for having led her that way at all. He of all people knew that simple questions weren't simple sometimes. They could detonate inside a person, rip through any semblance of stability and calm. Had he done that to her? Had he done her that harm?

He tried to look at her sideways, not call any more attention to his crime than he had to. She was holding her arms around her waist, keeping herself together. He hadn't blown her apart after all. She was hanging on. "I hate to think of you up on that slippery roof," she said. "I'll give you one more chance to back out, no questions asked, if you want me to call someone."

"Absolutely not," Jackson said. "I can't offer any references, but I have a pretty good idea of what needs to be done."

"Okay, I'm convinced." She had a quick, spontaneous laugh, full of energy, and it seemed to bring her back to herself. It delighted him to be the cause of it. Especially now when he had feared trespassing on her privacy, on whatever pain it was that she kept tamped down.

"Now, I'll need to make up a list of supplies." He examined the water-damaged ceiling of the corridor. "And there are some tools I'll need."

"Let me get you a pad to make your list," she said, hurrying downstairs.

Jackson wondered about her husband. Maybe he was away on business. If that, then he probably would make an appearance over the weekend. The roof was probably a two-day job if Jackson could get started this afternoon. With any luck, he could be packed up and gone by Friday night. Anyway, Jackson hoped he could, hoped he could get the roof work finished and be back on the road by then, driving away from the comfort of another man's wife.

Chapter 4

Every particle in the universe attracts every other particle
with a force that is directly proportional to both of
their masses and inversely proportional to the
square of the distance between them.

NEWTON'S LAW OF GRAVITATION

Jackson had a hypothesis he called the boomerang theory. You could only travel so far before you returned to face yourself. The universe is expanding near the speed of light, and it has been theorized that someday it will stop expanding and like a rubber band stretched as far as it will go, it will snap back. Gravity will assert itself and draw everything back to where it started. Physicists believe that when the universe stops expanding and begins to contract, the big bang will become the big crunch. Jackson's boomerang theory ran parallel to this idea. He always told Nancy that life could only get so bad and then it would reach the limits of the space-time continuum and flick backward like a ball on a string, turning better and better all the while. Of course, Jackson had never expected to dash up against the sharp outer edges of his emotional universe so soon, and lately he wasn't that certain about his pet theory anymore.

Still, he thought of it when Livvy offered to come with him to the hardware store. There was nothing more mundane than a trip to the hardware store, but he was unexpectedly surprised how much her offer pleased him. After spending so much time alone, trapped in the dizzying replay of his thoughts, he welcomed the company. Not just anyone's company—hers. And she, after a winter of isolation, sealed up in the inn with her books and the fireplace, seemed to want company herself. Certainly he could have found his own way to town, but Livvy told him she'd rather he not get lost on her account.

"Jackson," she had told him when he had finished making his list and had apologized for the expense it represented. "Taking care of this place is my job, it's been an ongoing labor of love for years now. Caretaking has to be, otherwise I don't know how anyone could do it."

She would be his first passenger in the Quark, and he gave her a guided tour. He deactivated the alarm, unlocked the side door, and invited her to step up into what had been his home since the summer before.

"Is this where you sleep?" she wondered, pointing to the narrow bunk with the foam mattress. His blue sleeping bag lay uncoiled on the mattress.

"It's not as comfortable as my bed at the inn, but when you're exhausted from the road, you could sleep on pavement," he said. "And I have a heater and a gas cooking stove."

"The curtains are a homey touch."

"Or homely," he corrected. "Bright green's never been my color, but you take the hand you're dealt."

"I think it's an ingenious way to travel," she said. "There's an efficiency to having everything you need right here. When we drove from Chicago, we were at the mercy of fast food and any roadside motel that had a vacancy."

"I stayed off the interstate when I could," Jackson said. "Usually, I drove one state highway into the next. Before I came north, I drove around the south for a while."

"Did you go to New Orleans? I just love that city."

Jackson groaned and nodded. "I drifted through this winter. It was Fat Tuesday, the traffic was unbelievable, and the Quark was threatening to overheat."

"It's such a romantic city," she said. "The streetcars, the magnolias, and the beignets."

"Ah, the beignets," Jackson nodded. "And the fried oyster po'boys. Those more than made up for my troubles."

"I used to live to travel," she said. "And after I met Howard, we went everywhere—San Francisco, New York, London, Paris, Rome," she said, wistfully.

"Where haven't you been yet?" Jackson asked. "Someplace you've always wanted to see?" He had never known pure wanderlust. There were family vacations, but he always couldn't wait to get back to the familiarity of home. Now he didn't know if he could ever bear going home.

Livvy closed her eyes for a moment and shook her head. "I don't know where I'd go," she said. "I can't even begin to imagine it now." She bent over to read the titles of his books. "Einstein, Stephen Hawking, Carl Sagan," she said. "Some impressive reading."

"Hazard of my profession," he said. She was dangerously close to the treasure of his photo albums on the shelf below.

"Well, you may actually be one of the few people who understands black holes and all those things."

"Sometimes," he admitted. Though there were whole days that passed when he felt that he might be the *only* person in the world really to understand. Black holes did not simply exist theoretically for Jackson; he felt as though he had lost his family to one. He knew that black holes only existed in deepest space, light-years away. They were the remains of gigantic stars that had imploded into themselves leaving only the ghosts of their gravitational fields, which could be detected by the anomalies they caused in the space around them. In theory, a passing spaceship might be innocently sucked into this angry vortex of gravity and never be heard from again. Its passengers would be torn into their most elementary particles by the tremendous gravitational forces within. Jackson had seen the evidence and reviewed the theories by scientists far more learned than himself.

Perhaps, he thought, on his days of more rational grief, the conjecture of physics could explain what had happened to his family. He could visit the graves, plant flowers, and run his hands over the polished granite stones, but what had happened to the essence of his children and his wife? He wondered idly if they had tumbled into some sort of ecclesiastical black hole. Maybe that's how it all worked. He certainly wouldn't have put it past nature to design things that way. In a universe ordered by unwavering law and punctuated by predictable interludes of chaos, he had to believe the essence of Nancy, Nathan, and Franny survived in some form, somewhere.

"Are these photo albums?" Livvy asked, bending low.

"Yes," Jackson said. He felt his stomach drop. He wasn't ready to provide answers to her curiosity, and braced for what he imagined would be her next probing question followed by the next— until his heart would explode like glass.

She ran her fingers over their spines, but she asked nothing else of him. It was enough for her to know what they were, and to allow him the distance of his privacy. He wished he had shown her the same courtesy in the attic.

"Shall we go?" she said, sounding pleased with what she had seen of his life in the Quark.

"Sure," he said. "Climb through to the front seat, if you want."

"Through here?"

"Yes," he said, guiding her with his hand. She edged over the hump of the transmission and came to rest in the passenger seat.

Jackson pulled the side door closed and jogged around to the driver's door and climbed in. The Quark started up with a hoarse, whining roar, which was the normal timbre of its voice. The vents on the dashboard buzzed and Jackson felt the fillings in his teeth vibrate. He tapped the shifter, and they were off.

"That's the Quark for you," he said. "It'll get you there—somehow."

"Why call it the Quark?"

"Because it's anything but," he said with a shrug. "A quark is a charged subatomic particle that comes in all different types— charmed, strange, up, down, top, and bottom. This old van can be all those flavors at once sometimes. Besides, it only has an AM radio and I needed to entertain myself somehow."

"It does have a mid-seventies high schoolish charm," she said, with a sarcastic giggle.

"Be kind," he warned playfully. "It's seen me through a lot of miles."

"Okay, I'll play tour guide now, if you don't mind."

"Please," Jackson replied.

"Well, anyone could tell you that's the public beach over there."

"Perfect for a long, head-clearing walk," Jackson added.

"Last summer, a whale beached itself just to this side of the jetty."

"I think I might have heard about it on the news," he said, recalling for an instant something similar, something familiar in the whole days lost to that numbing parade of electrons marching across the screen. After it had happened and he was alone, TV had become the only way he could slow the wild churning in his mind. He had sat rigid during the reports on the local stations about the man who had destroyed his family's life: the arrest, the reprehensible plea of his innocence. Sometimes Jackson could hear the hollow echo of that man's denial ringing in his own head, see the dead eyes that lay in his skull like stones, his potbelly that stretched his stained shirt wide. That was the beast that had caused Jackson's pain. And the TV camera had courted him.

"It was on all the networks," Livvy said. "Human interest story, I guess."

"Oh?" he said, his distraction consuming him.

"I've never seen such an enormous creature. It had beautiful, intelligent dark eyes. We were keeping his skin wet with seawater and I remember how rough it had felt dry, but as soon as the skin was wet it glided under your hands. Not slimy the way a fish at the market is, just frictionless. You can imagine how they just slip through the ocean."

"Did it ever get back into the water?"

"Oh yes, it took a tugboat that came from the harbor in Portland, but we got it out to sea again. It was very emotional."

They turned the corner of Beach Road and followed along a spit of land between the salt marsh and the harbor. There was a jogging path with a footbridge that spanned a creek trickling into the sea.

"And there, the Blue Gull Inn, which we almost bought," she said, pointing to a small inn with tennis courts facing the salt marsh. "Howard thought the beachfront property was a much better investment."

"Did you look at a lot of places?"

"Until I was dizzy," she said. "We drove up and down the coast trying to find just the right one. We both loved Rockpoint, so that was an easy choice. It was just a matter of finding what made us happy. After all, we were about to lay down our savings."

"You ended up with a beautiful place," he said. "The Victorian woodwork alone is magnificent."

"Would you believe that it was all painted white when we bought the inn? Howard and I stripped every inch of it, then we refinished it. We never would have known how beautiful it was if we hadn't stripped the paint off."

"You just have to wonder what people are thinking when they cover up detail like that."

Livvy directed Jackson to make a turn into town. They crossed a narrow drawbridge at the mouth of the harbor. There was a brightly painted shack selling fried fish that was just opening for the season at the near end of the bridge. Across the way was a short block of shops with their windows displaying T-shirts, porcelain lighthouses, and scrimshaw carvings done on ivory-colored plastic whale bone.

"Are you up for some lunch?" Livvy asked, tentatively.

"I was just thinking about that."

"I should have made us sandwiches back at the inn," she said.

"No, let me take you somewhere nice." He spoke with a quickness that even took him by surprise. He regretted it for a moment and tried to temper his words, but it was too late. He had allowed himself to fall into an easy, comfortable rhythm with her. It was as though they had suddenly become old friends. And it worried him.

Dominick's had a perfect view of the harbor with its clusters of working lobster boats and powerful fishing charters. The tables were hewn from heavy slabs of wood, thickly lacquered. There was a huge lobster tank with several dozen of the beasts piled on top of one another below the water. Thick braids of marine rope were coiled in decorative patterns on the wall. A tattered fishing net hung from one end of the ceiling. A graying man wearing a Greek fishing cap, his face lined as if chiseled into his hard face, greeted them at the door.

"Two for lunch today, Mrs. Faraday?" he asked, his voice rough with gravel.

"Yes, Dominick," Livvy said. "Will you be opening the outside deck soon?"

"Any day now, Mrs. Faraday," he said, leading them to a table by the window. "As soon as the weather cooperates."

"I guess we have to wait for the temperature to catch up with the calendar."

"As always," he said. "And how's your husband?"

"He's managing," she said. "I guess we all are."

"That's good," he said, warmly.

"This is a friend," she said, changing the subject deftly. "Jackson Tate." Dominick nodded and retreated into the cool shadows of the restaurant.

Jackson had a thick sandwich of grilled haddock on a huge toasted molasses cornmeal roll, while Livvy had a smoked seafood salad in a bed of baby lettuce. The boats in the harbor bobbed at their moorings and the sun warmed their table. Their conversation skimmed the surface for a long while, like a water skier. There was a natural flow to their words and ease in laughter that made Jackson feel that, indeed, they were old friends.

Without his even trying, the conversation turned the way of his curiosity. Livvy told him that she had left journalism school for a job at *Chicago* magazine, where she was writing when she met her husband. "I interviewed Howard for an article that I was writing for an issue on the city's best lawyers. We were always doing special issues like that because they sold so well. You know, the best doctors, the best places to eat, the best places to have your legs waxed."

"User friendly," Jackson said.

"It was such a racket, but that's another story," she said. "Anyway, one afternoon I went over to interview the master corporate deal-maker Howard Faraday at his office. And I thought he was charming, and very distinguished in his dark suit and silver hair. At the time, he was working for a firm and had won several big cases. He had just been asked to head up the legal department for some big conglomerate and everyone was very impressed. Well, our interview was supposed to last an hour, but he just kept talking right through dinner until I was too tired to take any more notes. I went back to my office, did some brief phone interviews with a few of his colleagues for background, and then the article came out a couple of weeks later."

"He must've loved it."

"He hated it," she said. "Absolutely hated it."

"They say some people just don't like reading about themselves."

"Well, that was Howard," she said with a gentle roll of her green eyes. "He said that even his picture made him look like someone's kind old uncle."

"Was there anything he liked about it at all?"

"Me, I guess," she said. "At the time, he told me in his booming, resonant voice, that same one he used to intimidate judges,

'Olivia, you have my deepest apologies, but your story set me back twenty-five years.' "

"How could that be?" Jackson asked.

"I wrote about him as I saw him—a reflective, intriguing man who loved fly-fishing and French wines."

"Ah, I get it," Jackson said. "No, lawyer ever wants to be seen as gentle."

"Exactly," she said. "I saw through that cocky lawyer artifice he wore, and I wrote about who was standing behind it. And that was not good for business. Not at all. He wanted to be seen as a shark."

"And how long after that was it until you got married?"

"Maybe a year or so," she said. "He joked that it was the only way to keep me from writing about him, either that or he'd have me transferred to *Siberian Monthly*."

"At least he gave you a choice."

"Ha!" she said. "Chicago winters are bad enough. Siberia." She shivered. "Forget about it."

"Aye, aye."

"How long have you been married, Jackson?" Her eyes alighted on the wedding band he still wore on his left hand.

The mood swung back into his face, slapped him. He was conscious of swallowing. "I *was* married," he said. Jackson felt the blood leave his face.

"Divorced?" Livvy said. She was trying to work some unruly lettuce onto her fork. She wasn't looking at him.

Jackson drew a breath sharply. "She was killed," he said as gently as he could. There wasn't another way to say it to soften the blow and he knew how information like that could grind the drive shaft of a conversation into dust.

Livvy looked up at him suddenly, white as he was. "I'm sorry," she apologized, obviously horrified to have stumbled into his sorrow in such a lackadaisical way. "So sorry."

He brushed aside her apologies and told Livvy that he had met Nancy while they were both in graduate school. They had been a two-degree family, he explained, his Ph.D. in physics and her master's of fine arts in dance. Even as he related the simple facts, he could see Nancy dancing with such quick-flowing movement it was like watching water tumble from a spring. It was in the darkness of a student theater that he had first seen her dance in the colored lights of the stage. His heart had quickened as he followed her motion. By the time he introduced himself at the wine-and-cheese gathering afterward, he was lost to her. But she was gone now, lost to him, maybe dancing somewhere in the light of the stars. He couldn't say all that to Livvy, of course, but it was the reality of his grief, of his life now: what he couldn't forget.

Livvy shook her head, pinched her lower lip. "What happened?"

"A drunk driver," he said, as though it could explain it all.

"That's heartbreaking," she said. Her hand moved toward his impulsively. She touched him lightly on the knuckles with her fingertips, then withdrew.

"What can I say?" he answered. "Matter impacts with antimatter all around us in billions and billions of atomic collisions every second."

"Some matter *matters* more, though, doesn't it?" she asked. "I mean, it has more meaning?"

He shrugged, then conceded, nodding. Of course.

"Is that why you left home?"

"Yes," he said softly. "I felt like I was drowning in memories. I suppose I still feel like that."

"Grief," she said, with gravity, "can overwhelm you."

Jackson explained how he had wanted to look for logical explanations and neat solutions. He told her a scientist needs to see a cause and effect and make order out of the seeming randomness of the world.

"Sometimes there is no answer," she said. "Or I don't think there is . . ."

He recalled for her a time when his son had asked him one of those questions kids always ask—why is the sky blue?—how he had launched into a complicated explanation. He had told Nathan about how the sun's light is scattered and absorbed by dust particles in the atmosphere and we see only the single blue spectrum of the light. And Nathan just stared at him, bewildered, and Jackson realized that his son didn't want to know the science behind it, he wanted to know the poetry of it. It was the science that Jackson saw, but it was the poetry that his son wanted to understand.

"And," he added, "I think about that sometimes. I know I have to learn to see things that way, rather than just as variables in some equation."

"Your son sounds like a smart kid," she said.

Jackson shifted in his seat uncomfortably. He should have been out with it, all at once. But he still couldn't bear the full burden of it, still had to parse it down into individual losses. Even now, he wasn't ready to say what he needed to tell her. It caught in his throat because he had never said those words aloud, and they had rung in his head all these months like the aftershock of a nuclear detonation. But Livvy had been kind to him, and he felt he had to be honest with her.

"My son . . ." he began, trying to smooth the knot in his throat. "My son was killed, too. In the same car wreck. And my daughter. She was two years old."

"Oh," Livvy said, though it was more of an exhalation than the forming of an actual sound. "I'm sorry. How awful for you, Jackson. I'm so sorry." She thumped her hand against her heart, as though the truly meaningful words she needed had lodged there and couldn't rise out of her to comfort him. She was mute with the truth.

He couldn't make himself look at her eyes. Sympathy was dangerous for him. "The police called it an accident. The impact killed them all instantly."

"I'm so sorry, Jackson," Livvy said. "How could you let me go on like that about Howard?"

"Really, at this point I'd rather hear about someone else's life." He tried to laugh, but he couldn't. "I mean, I've driven long enough thinking about what happened . . ."

"How old was your son?"

"Nathan was six."

"They were so young."

"My wife, Nancy, thought twice about naming our son Nathan," he said, the joke coming to him the way that Nancy used to tell it. "She said she didn't want him to grow up to be a weenie."

Livvy looked blank.

"You know, as in Nathan's hot dogs?" he said.

Livvy tried to laugh, but she couldn't force it either. And she was right. It wasn't funny anymore.

Jackson shrugged: "Nancy could make anything funny. And I know she would somehow have found some humor in what happened. God knows how, but she was like that. It was a saving grace." Jackson sighed. "Such a confluence of events. The law of probabilities. The alignment of vectors . . . I don't know what to make of it."

"You mean your heart is broken?" Livvy said.

"Yes," he said, nodding slowly. "Yes."

Chapter 5

In every energy transformation, some of the original energy is always changed into heat energy not available for further transformations.
THE SECOND LAW OF THERMODYNAMICS

Relief was what he felt as they left Dominick's and walked out onto the sidewalk into the spring sunshine. Certainly he was lighter. It surprised him to know that with nothing but words, flimsy words, he could give some of the burden to her—a moment of it, enough time to draw a breath.

It was relief tinged with guilt, though. The same sort of guilty acceptance that had settled in and lined his stomach with feathers when his father finally died after years of heart disease. His mother, a woman of mild emotion, grieved hard and long for her husband. In spite of their unhappiness together, she seemed to miss him, living in a small pastel-colored apartment on the Gulf Coast of Florida. Jackson had stayed with her for a while, when his journey brought him south. It surprised him how quickly her face had collapsed into age, how lines creased and furrowed into her skin. Her hair was more gray than brown and had grown coarse. She numbed herself with a simple routine—the hairdresser, the supermarket, an exercise class. The minutes and the hours of every week spiraled forward into the next, where the loop began again. An unscheduled hour might invite unscheduled thought, and the tug of grief could return to pull her downward.

They were quite a pair, Jackson and his mother. Lost in an echo of sighs as they rattled around her community, called Paradise Cove. Jackson bought Chinese takeout, and they sat on the couch with the food spread out on the coffee table and watched old episodes of *Columbo* and *Kojak* on cable. On other nights she cooked for him as she always had, dishes out of balance—pasta steely with raw garlic, chicken fiery with too much pepper, or a steak when he had given up red meat years ago after his father's first heart attack. They held fast to light subjects, as though they were skipping stones on the surface of conversation.

From his own dark pit of emotion, he feared for her. This new pain of losing her grandchildren and her daughter-in-law in one swift instant might take her down. She moved with a fragility that he wasn't accustomed to seeing. He came upon her in the laundry room one evening, waiting for the cycle to finish. She leaned against the machine with her back to him and when he saw her shoulders quaking, he thought for a moment that it was the machine agitating. But she was crying. He wanted to go to her or say something that would be of some comfort, but he didn't. Her grief was private, and he let her be, not because he didn't want to comfort her, but because he would have to tell her what he had done. Jackson would have to admit there was more to the tragedy, that her son, whom she had never thought capable of wrong-doing, was partly responsible. He was frozen with guilt.

Some families live as though they're in an Italian opera, splattering their troubles in all directions. The Tates, however, made certain to distance themselves from the impact of life's troubles. His parents never spoke of David Tate's heart problem, and when he was hospitalized for the last time, Jackson knew he wasn't coming home. But his mother never acknowledged it. Even at the funeral, after thirty years of marriage, she had a superhuman ability for holding herself together. She simply never shed a tear in front of anyone. Some would think she didn't care enough, but that wasn't true. Strong emotion had always shamed them, from an overwrought scene in the movies to the lenses of TV news broadcasts capturing people's trauma. Emotion was a foreign tongue that they had assiduously refused to learn.

Jackson recalled once, when he was a seven-year-old boy and walking with his father in Manhattan, they had come upon a woman who had just jumped from a high apartment window. Her body was splayed across the sidewalk on her side, blood trickled from her head, and one eye was opened in an expression that Jackson could only describe as surprise. His father gasped, but made no attempt to shield his boy's eyes from the unexpected horror. She must have just hit the ground; in fact, Jackson recalled hearing a hollow-sounding thud before they turned the corner.

"Oh my god! Oh my god!" a doorman shouted, as he ran flat-footed from the building. He stopped short of the widening pool of blood and looked up at Jackson and his father. "Oh my god!" he said again.

A crowd gathered, traffic stopped, and taxi drivers leaned out their cab doors. An ambulance had been called, and after some time they heard sirens. Jackson's father remained motionless, as if he were overcome by some strange inertia. Sweat gathered on the skin above his lip. The woman was gathered together and rolled onto the ambulance. A police officer with a belly that tumbled over his belt took a statement from the doorman. When a maintenance worker finally turned on a hose to wash the blood and brains from the sidewalk, Jackson tugged on his father's arm. There was no response, and he tugged again.

"What?" his father snapped. He glared at Jackson, with a look that nearly withered him to the concrete like a crushed dandelion. The show was over, the crowd had dispersed, but still, David Tate stood stiffly. He snorted, then pressed his lips together so hard they disappeared. A moment of fear, sadness, or horror was enough to shut down the synapses of the Tates. The extremity of life caught them off guard, rendered them wide-eyed in disconnected isolation. This common sensitivity to the glare of the emotional spotlight is perhaps what united the Tates—until Jackson met Nancy.

"I don't know whether they feel things more intensely than anyone else, or if they don't feel at all," he remembered her saying as they drove away from the hospital where his father lay dying. "But if that were my parents in there, saying good-bye, you couldn't pry them apart for anything."

"They just don't know how to express themselves," Jackson said, reaching for any explanation at hand.

"But how did you turn out like you?" Nancy said. "You're always saying that you love me."

"Maybe it's a mutated gene," he said. "I'm the first Tate to loosen up." He laughed hollowly. "It's just that I understand their world and I can shuttle back and forth."

"Well, I couldn't stand it if either of us were less than one hundred percent involved." She reached across the car to him. They had been married less than a year and had driven cross-country during the university's winter break to stay with his mother after his father's heart failed.

Nancy had tried repeatedly to unravel the Tates' tight emotional loop, but she never got far. After David Tate's death,

Jackson's mother still lived as if her husband were coming home on the 5:52 train, burning big meals of pot roast and potatoes for dinner. But the grief she had choked down escaped in insidious ways. She began to fall, tripping on the walkway and bruising her knee, or losing her footing on the granite steps of the post office. She bruised, sprained, twisted, and finally broke a wrist chasing after a runaway shopping cart in the supermarket parking lot. That's when they convinced her she needed to start a new life. She chose Florida because she liked the warm weather.

Jackson couldn't mourn his Nancy and Nathan and Franny in such quiet depression. That part of him that Nancy had recognized and loved him for wouldn't let him. His anger at their deaths built a fire of rage inside him. He tried to live by his mother's rhythms while he was with her, but he felt as though he were being snuffed out. Finally, he had to be on his own again.

"Sometimes I just don't know how you got out of there alive," Nancy told him once when they left his mother after a visit. "It's like living in the vacuum of space."

Jackson didn't argue. Given his upbringing, it was natural that he gravitated to the safety of a world of inclined planes and predictable van der Waals forces. If it hadn't been for Nancy, he never would have known any other way. He knew that she had made him understand what it means to hold someone and be held. Love flowed between them like a liquid, and held them up, the two of them skating on it like insects on a pond.

Nancy had once told him, "Everyone has to find something to take comfort in."

And Jackson had replied, "Then I take you."

But she was gone now.

In front of the restaurant, they climbed into the Quark and Livvy began to give him directions to the building-supply store out on Route 1. They drove slowly through the quiet town, which Livvy had told him became so traffic-clotted in the summer that she preferred to ride her bicycle. At the drawbridge next to the fried clam stand, the Quark did something it had done a thousand times before: it sputtered. Jackson gave the engine a little more gas to keep it from stalling, and there was suddenly a whoosh that sounded like lighter fluid on hot barbecue coals. Black smoke billowed out from under the hood, and there was the lick of orange flame over the windshield. Jackson watched stunned for an instant, until Livvy roused him.

"Get out," she yelled over the steady roar of the flames. She jumped out of the passenger side and backed up onto the sidewalk.

Jackson ignored her panic and made a dash through the cabin of the Quark. He snapped off the elastic shock cord that fastened across the lower shelf where he kept the photo albums. He scooped up the three thick albums in his arms and pulled them to safety, throwing open the latch on the side door. The flames and smoke arced over the top of the Quark. He set the photo albums on the sidewalk and turned to race back for the other essentials.

"Jackson!" Livvy shouted. She grabbed his arm.

"Just a few more things," he said, raising an arm in front of his face to shield him from the intense heat.

She didn't let go of his arm. "Wait, please. You have what was most important." Her hands wrapped tight around to hold him.

"I know, I know," he said, but the words caught in his throat as he watched the Quark swathed in flame.

The Rockpoint Fire and Rescue volunteers hosed down the vehicle with a thick flame-retardant foam. They didn't want to risk spreading the oily flames by using water. Globs of foam, like whipped cream, dropped through the steel drawbridge grate and into the harbor water below. A front tire popped and deflated from the heat. Jackson held the albums to his chest and watched silently. Livvy's arm was curled around his, and she pressed against him. He leaned into the softness of her shoulder, and it calmed the adrenaline that pumped through his body, racing his heart. A volunteer paramedic, whom Jackson recognized as a busboy from the restaurant, asked if they were all right.

"Looks like you have a few minor burns there," the paramedic pointed out.

Jackson looked at the backs of his hands. There were spots of soot and a few stinging red marks. The paramedic led him over to the back of the ambulance, and Jackson sat on a low step at the rear door while his burns were cleaned and dressed with a sterile pad. They were nothing, but he let the paramedic practice.

The flames were finally smothered, and the firemen began to reel hoses back onto the trucks. The chief came over to interview Jackson about the fire.

"There's nothing to tell, really," he said, his voice tight with shock. "The thing just went. Call it spontaneous combustion."

The fire chief radioed the service station across the street for a tow truck. "We've got to open up this lane to traffic," he said. His helmet had slipped low over his eyes and the collar on his heavy coat was flipped up.

"Nothing like witnessing thermodynamics in action," Jackson said to Livvy, shaking his head. The tow-truck driver pulled up and worked some levers to hoist the Quark onto a flatbed. The driver pulled himself up into the cab for the short trip back to the service station. Jackson and Livvy walked the half block in silence. His humiliation stung more than the burns on his hand. His life was already in a state of free fall, and he supposed it made some warped sense that everything he came in contact with should follow in its collapse.

At the service station, the Quark was lowered into a space behind the garage. Jackson began to climb through the still-hot wreckage to gather his possessions. He stacked a few singed books and grabbed his art supplies. Reaching under the burnt front seat for his toolbox, he burned his hand again on the hot metal. The fumes from melted plastic wafted out and the tattered rag that had been cut from a pair of his son's worn flannel pajamas had been blackened by the heat.

They got a ride back to the inn from the fire chief. Sammy was a stocky guy with a flat, expressionless face that only became animated when he laughed a cigarette-hoarse laugh. Jackson thought he looked like a bulked-up Buster Keaton. They rode three across in his pickup truck down Beach Road as Jackson balanced the remains of his belongings on his lap.

Inside the inn, Jackson followed Livvy to the bar, where she poured two glasses of wine for them.

"I think we both could use a drink now," she said, handing him a glass.

"I don't know what happened," he said. "The fuel line could have worn. I knew I should have replaced it. I've driven the Quark twenty thousand miles and it was already broken down."

"Well, whatever it was, I guess Rockpoint is where it wanted to give up the ghost," she said.

"I can't believe how fast the heat and flames wiped everything out. If the fire department hadn't been as fast as they were, it could have been worse."

"I'll have to remember to make a larger Christmas donation this year," she said dryly.

"I'm not so sure I'd want to have more than my hand bandaged by a busboy," Jackson added.

"That's the beauty of an all-volunteer squad. The person who does your hair in the morning is the same one working the Jaws of Life to extract you from your car."

Jackson took a long swallow of wine. For an instant, as those flames had leapt up around them in the Quark, he had a flash of what it might have been like for Nancy and the kids. The panic had nearly immobilized him. If Livvy hadn't been there to shake him from his stupor, he might have just sat in the driver's seat of the Quark. He might have let those flames consume him. He thought of the way the dashboard had begun to melt and deform from the heat. The windshield had shattered into a network of fine cracks running like a transparent road map across the sky.

He had felt the heat on his legs, curling the fine dark hair under his cotton pants. The fumes washed into his nose and over his clothes, as though he himself were soaked in gasoline. He imagined how his clothes might have burned and the smell of it all climbing up through the air. He would have clamped on hard to the steering wheel as the pain finally reached him. The gold band on the finger of his left hand, which he had not taken off since Nancy had slipped it on his finger seven years ago, would have melted into a puddle the color of the sun. They were so young when they married, it seemed to him now, and were too deep into their studies to take more than a hurried, weekend honeymoon. To make up for it, they had tried to live as if they were perpetually on honeymoon. Sometimes, if they were being particularly tender to each other in public, strangers asked them if they were newlyweds. It happened long after their two children had been born. That was just the way they were.

God help him, he would have sat in that damn vehicle until the flames had sizzled the fat on his bones. Like the pictures of the saffron-robed monks he had seen setting fire to themselves in Asia. He imagined that he would have let that fire tear through every flammable inch of the Quark, swallowing his prized photos and finally him. The straight-back brown vinyl seat with the spring that had poked him in the back would hold Jackson's greasy ashes. It would become his funeral pyre, and the smoke that rose up from his smoldering bones would rise straight up in the air like a bullet, gathering speed over towns and cities. Streaming like a supersonic mist over the back roads that he had traveled. Whirling through the house in Illinois with the bikes in the driveway and the vegetable garden in back. And somehow, this smoky atomic essence of Jackson Tate would be propelled into the inky black of space to return to the family he so loved.

The phone rang abruptly and he was jolted out of his dark thoughts. Livvy ran into the lobby to answer it. He heard her speaking in low tones, but the urgency in her voice was unmistakable. Her fragile eyes looked injured when she returned.

"Is everything okay?" Jackson asked.

"This is turning into quite a day." She sighed and looked at her watch. "I'll be back in a while. Make yourself at home."

He wanted to press her for a more satisfying response to his concern, but he let it go. He didn't have the energy to pursue those mysteries. He was still trying to unravel his own. But he had already tacked together a loose framework of possibilities that hung in space like those models of molecules they used in the chemistry department at the university. At the center of it all, he suspected, was Livvy's husband, Howard.

But it wasn't his business, he reminded himself. He was only passing through town. His heart felt for Livvy, though. The unexpected phone calls, the concern for her in town—it all led to a place of sorrow. And he wasn't so lost in his own sadness that he couldn't see hers. It concerned him that he was worried for her and that he could see how she craved some kind of comfort, as he did. It was concern that competed with his thoughts for Nancy and the children. And he wished he could just dismiss it, since it implied that he cared for Livvy when he thought he was past ever caring again.

Jackson watched her car pull away through a part in the lace-curtained windows. He waved with a quick turn of his bandaged hand.

Chapter 6

Only two possibilities exist: either one must believe in
determinism and regard free will as a subjective illusion, or
one must become a mystic and regard the discovery of natural
laws as a meaningless intellectual game. Ordinary people
have always accepted the dual nature of the world.

MAX BORN (1882–1970)

Alone that afternoon, Jackson's mind roiled, and he walked to the
beach across the street to try to clear his head. He had learned to
live with his restlessness, walking it off or distracting himself when
he could. But at the worst moments, at moments like this, he
thought he might never forgive Nancy. He might never forgive

her for teaching him how to recognize his own deepest feelings—
and then leaving him alone with them. He had needed her most
when she was lost to him forever. He needed her now.

You are insignificant, he told himself. *You are small.* He thought of
the universe around him, expanding like a big breath. He imagined the time, tens of billions of years in the future, when the universe would stop expanding and begin slowly cinching inward in
a prolonged contraction. The arrow of time that has propelled us
forward into the future would swing around and travel in reverse,
bringing us back to the past. It was one theoretical end to the wild
entropic crumbling of the universe. In time, he mused, his family
might be intact again, living their lives in reverse—dying before
they were born, growing younger instead of aging. He imagined
living his grief all over again, the tears rolling up his cheeks and
flowing back into his eyes. But in a wild theoretical sense, it would
mean he could have his family back again.

He found a driftwood log on the beach and sat, letting the
sand roll over the toes of his shoes. Overhead, there was the pierc-
ing cry of gulls and the wail of the wind as it tousled his hair. There
was always wind at the shore, any shore. They had visited the
ocean with the kids to see the town on a back inlet of Chesapeake
Bay, where Nancy had grown up. He knew that she missed the
rhythm of its tides. Maybe, he thought sometimes, that's where
she drew her inspiration for her dance. The dancers in her chore-
ographed pieces seemed to move like waves across the stage. They

crossed in undulating rhythms and flowed like the sea-flooding tidal flats.

On a family vacation they once drove far into the West, crossing the great windy expanse of the Dakotas and into the rising peaks of Montana. The wind blew hard there too, skimming over a clear lake that wore the reflection of the snowy Rockies that rimmed its shore like a crown. They swam in the crystal waters of a lake in Glacier National Park. The water was so clear that Jackson could see his wife dive below him to reach for a handful of smooth pebbles from the bottom. They swam while Nathan sat on the shore, raking stones into a pile with his fingers. Franny wasn't born yet; she was just a name they had planned on using someday. The water was cold as melted snow, and the air that day had been so thick with heat, they figured even the bears were too lazy to leave the shade of their dens.

The wind was gathering strength and they had heard it first in the tops of the pines. And slowly it dropped to ripple the water of the lake. As they swam into shore, it stirred whitecaps from the water. The towels that lay on the rocky shore whipped like flags in the air. In the sky above, clouds marched across the blue. They took shelter in the car, dripping and shivering. There, they unwrapped sandwiches for lunch and ate as the whirlwind of an approaching thunderstorm rocked the car. He recalled feeling that they were a family, a completed circle, protective of one another, and huddled together against the elements.

Jackson and Nancy had built something new and fabulous to him. He instinctively knew there was more to being a family than just sharing the same last name, but it had taken so long for him to understand. So much of himself needed to be left behind, tainted by the psychic radiation of his own birth family gone awry.

His parents had been content in the comfort of suburban New York. For them, all they needed was contained in the few square miles of their town that was linked to Manhattan by the capillaries of rail and road. His father commuted, and Jackson stayed at home with his mother. Their lives only intersected at mealtimes and had a routine that hardly wavered. On Sunday nights, when his mother was tired of cooking, Jackson would drive with his father to pick up a pizza at Mario's. The restaurant was plastered in white stucco, there were map-of-Italy paper placemats on the tables, and colored lights illuminated a tank with gray-colored fish that looked overfed and lazy. His father and he had stayed and eaten at Mario's a few times, plodding through a crust of melted cheese covering a dish of lasagna or parmigiana. Other times, riding home in the car, Jackson held the hot pizza box on his lap and felt it burn into his thighs. When he couldn't stand it anymore, he raised the box and held it an inch or two above his legs. A yeasty, oregano-and-basil-tinged smell filled the car. The steam fogged the window. Once, on the way home from just such an outing, the pizza burning hot in his lap, Jackson idly asked his father a question.

"Dad? How much do you get paid?"

His father turned slowly to him, his eyes suddenly burning like the pizza in Jackson's lap. "What?"

"Nothing," Jackson said, realizing that he had stepped over the line.

"It's none of your business what I get paid," his father snapped. He laughed at the incredulity of it all. "What possible reason would you have for asking me that kind of question?"

"Forget it," he said. "I didn't think."

His parents lived their lives with a creeping secrecy that was smothering. It was clear that David Tate earned a comfortable living with a reputable firm, but maybe it was the years of having to watch his back in a competitive office that had turned him. There was a streak of paranoia as wide as the Hudson River that simply made whole aspects of his life unmentionable. Jackson never knew when an idle comment or question was going to inspire his vitriol. David Tate was well known for his extremes, gentleness or volcanic fury. There were his rants about the neighbor's fence lines or an outburst of temper at a supermarket cashier. But there was also the David Tate who could behave with a gentle kindness, and he missed that. Over time, Jackson's mother had fully assimilated his father's anxiety, perhaps she had even contributed some of her own. She had insisted that Jackson's grade reports, clothing sizes, and IQ were all protected family secrets. Jackson took out his frustration in his studies, but even when he brought home A's and perfect scores on college entrance exams, he felt like there was no one to tell.

He stumbled shyly into an internship during his sophomore year in high school that opened an escape hatch. Through his school science department he applied to work at a major research lab in the city. He did not know the intricacies of physics yet, but he was content to assist in whatever he could do. During the week, after school, he rode the train thirty minutes into the city and walked across town to a research hospital. Jackson worked with a radiologist who was coordinating a long-term research project. The internship paid a stipend for his travel expenses, but the work was dull, full of numbers and graphing. At six o'clock, he met his father at his office and they walked across the street to Grand Central Terminal.

On a snowy evening, David Tate called the lab to tell Jackson he would have to work late. Jackson had already left and his boss, Dr. de Leon, answered the phone. Dr. de Leon was Argentinean, with the softly handsome features of a movie star. He must have talked to Jackson's father for a while, because when Jackson arrived at David's office, he was still flushed from conversation.

"I just got off the phone with your boss," his father said. He was beaming as he pushed himself out from behind his gray steel desk. A bookshelf on the wall displayed the latest corporate reports and photographs of Jackson and his mother. There was the stub of a cigar in a heavy glass ashtray on the desk. "Dr. de Leon thinks pretty highly of you."

"I don't know what for," Jackson said, modestly. "All I do is track data and graph it."

"There's more to it than that." He gestured for Jackson to sit in one of the blue vinyl upholstered desk chairs. "First of all, he says you're doing a wonderful job. Second—and I hope you can take a compliment—he thinks you're a pretty smart guy. Of course I could have told him that." His father smiled broadly.

"There's a lot to learn."

"And he says you're doing it beautifully. He wanted to know if you planned on pursuing the sciences. He went on and on about you and of course I didn't mind listening."

"I don't know." Jackson wasn't sure yet which science he would specialize in. All he knew was that his father's rich words made him edgy.

"Next year you should ask him for a college recommendation," David Tate said. "A good word from a top guy like him should carry some weight."

"Sure, Dad," he said.

His father was buoyant with this moment of unexpected praise, as if the words had come from his own boss. It made Jackson feel good for a different reason, though, not because of the things that de Leon had said about him, but for the way his father was talking to him.

"That's good," David Tate said. "I always told you to stand up for yourself and pull your weight in the world. Just keep doing exactly what you're doing and you'll be fine."

Jackson called home to tell his mother that they would be eating dinner in the city. Then, tossing his work aside, David Tate took his son out for a steak dinner at a dark wood–paneled clubby restaurant with red linen tablecloths. They sat in leather banquettes at a table in a back corner. Their steaks were as large as their plates, with potatoes like softballs. It was a celebration—because his father's new opinion of him opened the door for Jackson's autonomy. Finally, he could begin to pull away.

Jackson stood on the coast of Maine and brushed the sand from the seat of his cotton chinos. He hiked back up toward the inn. The sunset cast a pinkish orange glow across the sky. He peeled the adhesive tape and gauze that the paramedic had wrapped around his hand and saw that his injury was no worse than a sunburn. He balled the dressing up and wadded it into his pocket.

The Quark had given Jackson his freedom, and now it was wrecked. He was trapped. But anyway Jackson had found no comfort in his travels. He had tried to follow his father's instructions: He had looked out for himself. But even he could recognize that the fast food restaurants he had driven through and the rest stops he had napped at were no place for someone mired in grief.

Inside Livvy's inn, he poked around the cramped kitchen. It was the size of an airplane galley, but it had all the necessary tools. There was a small commercial range and a shelf full of pots and pans. Livvy was still away, and he looked around carefully, as if she might return at any moment. The small refrigerator was stocked with enough ingredients to put together a minor feast. He took a quick inventory of the groceries she had bought that morning and let his imagination work. It had been a long time since he'd done any cooking that required more than a bowl and a can opener. But he and Nancy had loved to cook together. It revived them out of the exhaustion of their workdays to cook a meal together. Sometimes she played sous-chef to him, and often they reversed their roles, with Jackson chopping ingredients for her creations. Maybe a turn in a well-stocked kitchen would be the nourishment his soul craved.

There was a fresh chicken in the refrigerator and he washed it clean in the porcelain sink. He dismembered it expertly, and set a sauté pan on the Viking range, adjusting the gas to lick up around the sides. He browned the chicken pieces, then reduced the heat and covered the pan. As the chicken cooked, he went to the bar and selected a California white wine for dinner from the rack and set it on ice. In the kitchen, he took a bag of fresh shrimp from the refrigerator and a crock of Greek black olives. In the pantry he found the other ingredients he needed. When the chicken was ready, he removed the pieces from the pan and began composing the sauce with onions, wine, chicken stock, herbs, and tomato paste. He stood over the stove stirring the sauce he had made for the chicken and inhaling the heady aroma of wine and herbs. There was a familiar pulse that had returned to him in the chemistry of combining ingredients. He had nearly forgotten the gentle pleasure of chopping onions and herbs, but it returned to him easily. The warm smells of the kitchen stirred his memories. He had missed this dearly.

He had cooked for Nancy soon after they met. He had been teaching himself to bake then, testing yeasts and sourdoughs, kneading dense loaves of pumpernickel and wheat. The kitchen was simple, just an alcove in a small grad-student apartment near the university, but his technique compensated for what he lacked in equipment. He approached it like a scientist: When his loaves were coming out too dense, he doubled their rising time and monitored the temperature of the oven with a heat-proof thermometer he had borrowed from the lab. He did think of it as an experiment, but a soothing one, and at a certain point, he was feeling that way about Nancy too.

For a month they had pursued each other, but shyly. There had been long walks and bike rides down country roads lapped on either side by cornfields. There had been concerts in the park and lunches on the lawn by the library. But there had been no touching at all. It was strange for him, a relationship that was all about what they had to say and not what her skin would feel like or what it would be like to taste her mouth. So when Jackson decided to cook a meal for Nancy, he didn't know what lay ahead, he only knew he was moving toward some kind of love he had never known before, had never even expected could exist. He asked her to dinner because they had seen all the movies in a twenty-mile radius and he didn't want a Friday night to pass without seeing her and because he knew already that she was going to mean something to him, was going to *be* something to him.

He thought Nancy must be a vegetarian—weren't all dancers?

But he wasn't sure and was too embarrassed to ask, since he should have noticed before, but they had always eaten pizza or shared a late-night grilled cheese after the movies. So he played it safe. He made a honey whole wheat dough and let it rise while he taught a two-hour lab for an undergrad physics course. He divided the dough and rolled it out. Into each round, he spooned tomatoes, peppers, onions, broccoli, and garlic that he had rendered into sweetness by sautéing in olive oil and finishing with a splash of wine. He grated fresh Parmesan and mozzarella over it, folded the dough in half, and pinched the edges closed. Then he set the calzone in the oven.

Nancy arrived just as he was melting the chocolate for the dessert he was going to bake for her. She had walked the few blocks from the campus, and he could smell the autumn wind in her hair, see it in the blaze of her cheeks. "Chocolate," she said, sniffing the air and picking that scent out despite the onions and the baking bread dough of the calzones. "How did you know that it's my favorite?" (He hadn't.) She had brought a bottle of cheap red wine, from Algeria or some other place that was known more for its secret police than its vineyards, and they laughed about it and poured it with dinner. And though she complimented the meal, especially the crust, she kept asking about dessert, eager for it. The aroma of the chocolate was everywhere, tantalizing.

When he unmolded the tiny cakes from their buttered ramekins, she hugged him suddenly, seizing him up with her own anticipation. Chocolate was a passion for her. He sprinkled powdered sugar on each of the two cupcake-sized desserts and she lifted a dense spoonful to her mouth. "It's like eating a chocolate cloud," she said. "What do you call them?"

"Raspberry chocolate mousse cakes," he said.

"You're a delight," she said, making a show of sighing her contentment.

"It's my pleasure," he said. And it had been. There was a dab of chocolate in the corner of her mouth. He leaned toward her before he could lose his nerve and kissed her there. She turned her head in surprise and kissed him back. They kissed again.

Later, when they were married, she teased him that that was the moment things turned. She had been nervous, afraid to commit to him, but when he cooked for her, everything changed. She had to marry Jackson, she told their children later, because he wouldn't turn loose of that recipe she loved so much. Part of the private wedding vows they made up on their honeymoon provided that they would share that dessert on every anniversary. And they hadn't missed a single one. He always baked the raspberry chocolate mousse cakes; she always said, "Oh, good, it's time for the chocolate clouds."

Livvy came in through the back door of the kitchen just as he was peeling the shrimp. Her eyes looked downcast and defeated. Her lips were set in a solemn expression. As soon as she saw what Jackson was doing, the brightness returned to her face.

"Oh you didn't!" she said.

"It's the least I can do after nearly blowing us up," Jackson said. "Besides, I didn't notice any signs about guests not using the kitchen."

"You can use the kitchen anytime if you're going to make it smell like this," she said. "What are you cooking? I'm starving."

"Napoleon's chef called it chicken marengo. I call it one of the few recipes I know by heart."

"Chicken marengo," she said. "I'm amazed."

"I intend to replace what I've used, of course."

"Don't be ridiculous," she said.

He sautéed the shrimp and set them aside. "I'm coming into the homestretch now."

"Anything I can do to help?"

"You can just get ready to eat." Jackson sliced rounds of crusty French bread and sautéed them in the splash of oil he had used to cook the shrimp. In simmering water, he poached four eggs. He tossed the chicken pieces in the sauté pan with the tomato sauce and onions to warm them, then arranged it all on a plate. He surrounded the chicken with the four jumbo shrimp placed at equal intervals, then between the shrimp he positioned toasted rounds of French bread, and finally arranged a poached egg on each piece of toasted bread. It looked like a solar system on a plate, with eggs and shrimp orbiting a sun-colored chicken.

"Voilà, chicken marengo," Jackson said. He carried the dish to the dining room, where Livvy had set the table with a tablecloth and two candles. The silverware gleamed in the candlelight. He served them both and sat down.

"How was your day?" he said, play-acting to disguise his melancholy mood. "Not counting the fiery demise of my truck, of course."

"I'd have to say this is the highlight." She laughed and began to eat. "This is wonderful. Do you cook like this on the road?"

He shook his head and laughed. "Actually, I haven't cooked in a very long time," he said. "I've prepared plenty of food on the road, but none of it has been what I would call cooking."

"Food is my greatest solace," she said.

Jackson nodded and lifted his wine in agreement.

"There's something so restorative about a wonderfully cooked meal." She set down her fork. "Thank you, Jackson. This is the kindest thing anyone's done for me in a long time."

"Thank *you*," he said. "For the company. And the nicely stocked kitchen."

"Any time," she said. "There are few greater pleasures in life than being cooked for."

"I'll agree with that," he said. He had cooked for himself, but he was glad that it had boosted her spirits, too.

"Howard introduced me to gourmet cooking," she said. "Whenever we traveled, he loved to arrange a day around a meal. We'd visit the cathedral at Chartres and then race back to Paris for the first seating at some wonderful place with a constellation of Michelin stars." She sighed long. There was bitterness in it.

But he found he couldn't ask.

They ate for a long while in silence. She sipped from her wineglass and smiled at him, looking so deeply into his eyes that he felt them ache. It shamed him, somehow. He had cooked tonight to feel closer to Nancy and soothe himself, but suddenly he worried that Livvy had misunderstood, that he would hurt her more than she already was. He wanted to warn her away, wanted to make her see how she had tapped into some current in him that was alive with his lost family. She was merely a catalyst. "Livvy," Jackson said, slowly, "the worst thing about today wasn't the van burning."

"Tell me," she said. Her eyes were tender, unguarded.

"I've been trying to escape," he said, the depth of his emotion taking him by surprise. "But I can't, anymore. I haven't spoken about them to anyone since it happened. Until I did with you, today."

She looked down at the table and shook her head ever so slightly.

"Somehow," he said. "I feel they're alive in me again. Because you're the first person I've allowed into the same places. I don't mean to embarrass you . . . but your kindness. I feel them more than I have in a long time. And I don't know if what I'm feeling is a blessing or a curse . . . remembering."

After a long moment, her eyes locked on his again. There was resolve in them, a steeliness. "It's a blessing," she said emphatically. "My husband can't remember anything about the years we've had together. He can't remember my name, or the word for the color of my eyes."

It was at that moment, that Jackson curled his hand over hers. Or she had moved toward him, he wasn't sure. It was a reflex. Two people, nearly strangers, their futures cast in doubt and their pasts full of pain, had reached for the comfort of each other. As they sat there, wordless, one of the candles burned down to a trickle of wax that ran down the crystal candlestick. The flame flickered madly, then finally slipped into the melted wax pooled in the base of the candlestick, and sizzled out. Livvy squeezed Jackson's hand and let her fingers lace with his. In the light of the remaining candle, he could see the way the green in her eyes shimmered, as though she might be about to cry. "Emerald," he thought. "Emerald is the color of your eyes."

Chapter 7

*The acceleration that a net force gives an object is directly
proportional to the magnitude of the force and
inversely proportional to the mass of the object; the
acceleration is in the direction of the applied force.*

NEWTON'S SECOND LAW OF MOTION

From the rooftop Jackson could see from one end of Beach Road
to the other. He could even make out the stubby steel frame of the
drawbridge in town, painted a creamy colonial white. At sea, there
was a vessel that was nothing more than a dark rise on the horizon, the low hull of a tanker maybe. A sailboat came around the
point, its main sails luffing in the changing wind. Livvy had been

guarded that morning, professional in demeanor, hurrying out on errands with hardly a word to Jackson, and later there would be rooms to ready for the Memorial Day reopening. She was busy.

Waking, he had hoped things wouldn't be awkward between them after that candlelit moment the night before. He had hoped that it hadn't bred expectation, that twining of hands and sharing of stories. It had been such a spontaneous intimacy, so of the moment. Lying in bed the morning after, he regretted it.

That feeling was hastily extinguished by her aloofness, by her disappearance just after breakfast. True, he didn't want her to expect anything of him. But he had come already to expect something of her: that easy companionship of the day before, the warmth of her presence, the relief in finding someone to listen. He didn't want to give that up. Not after so long without it.

Selfish, he acknowledged. But then it had been a long time since he had indulged himself. It had been a long time since there was anything or anyone even to tempt him to self-indulgence. What was it in her that had made him want to be near her when he had spent so many months fleeing other people?

At least there was work to turn his hands to. Maybe his mind would follow. He stood on an extension ladder he had dragged from the garage, examining the damaged slate pieces on the roof. The gray slate could hold up for decades, solid and watertight, but it was as fragile as a pane of glass under certain conditions. A branch from a twisted old maple tree had come down on the roof in a windstorm and battered the slate hard in half a dozen places. It was brittle enough to flake and crack. But Jackson knew he could fix it. He was used to repairing houses.

In the summer after his senior year of high school, before he went off to college, Jackson had put in two months with the crew of a local contractor. The work paid nicely, and he needed the money for school. He wanted to work outside of a lab internship, which he knew he could get easily, but where the token salaries they would pay him could hardly cover his expenses. Besides, he wanted to get out in fresh air that wasn't filtered for particles and scrubbed by activated charcoal. Most of all, he wanted to earn some real money before he went off to school.

That summer he learned to sweat through his clothes and guzzle cans of cheap beer to cool himself at the end of the day. The work was harder than any he had ever done, but it was Jackson's first chance to earn a workingman's wage. After his first day wielding a hammer, he could hardly move his arms. After his first week, he noticed biceps and shoulders developing so that his T-shirts fit more snugly. It was what he wanted to do, knowing he would enter the world of academia in the fall. His father objected, of course, to Jackson's blue-collar stint.

"Science is learning how things work," Jackson had told him, while devouring a stack of pancakes one Sunday morning at the Neptune, a Greek diner with a six-page menu where they now went together. Day or night you could order anything from eggs to lobster Newburg. It was built where the chrome soda fountain of Joe's once stood.

"So learn how things work where you can get some relevant experience," his father said. "I can help you with pocket money when you're in school."

"It's not about that," he said. "The only way I can learn is to do it myself. Next summer, I might want to work on cars at a garage. It's applied science."

"Jesus Christ, Jackson," his father said. He kneaded his forehead with his pink fingertips.

"That's not what I'm going to do forever," he promised his father. "I just don't want to be one of those people who can just do one thing."

David Tate pinched his thin lips together and picked up his mug of coffee. His brow darkened. Jackson knew his father's temper was working inside, simmering like a steam engine. He knew how explosive it could be, since he had seen glimmers of the same temper residing within himself. They said no more about the construction work.

All that summer Jackson had balanced fat bundles of shingles on his shoulders and climbed ladders, or hammered two-by-fours, or endured the monotony of house painting. Jackson was the college boy who got all the grunt work, but he didn't mind that. It gave him the distance to observe. He watched how the electricians ran the wiring to the fixtures and into the circuit box. He helped the plumber run copper pipe through the bathrooms and solder the lengths together. It was an education he absorbed.

The contractor who owned the outfit was a stocky goon with a thick, tangled head of brown hair. His mustache draped lazily over his lips and he kept his substantial belly filled with a diet of cider doughnuts, takeout pizza, and Bud. He had been a roofer for years, and that was his specialty. It had ruined his knees, though, crawling around pounding nails through shingles and plywood sheathing. So he had moved into remodeling work that he could do standing upright—barely. His knees had been so ravaged that he couldn't seem to stand steady for more than a moment. He would lean and weave in place, grabbing at a stud wall to steady himself, then show off the long pink trails of his surgical scars, like parentheses around his kneecaps. After a while, Jackson wondered if his boss's unsteadiness wasn't just from dipping into the stocked cooler in his truck whenever the thirst struck him.

There was a lot Jackson learned that summer, besides how to pad a bill. It was the experience he needed that gave him the confidence some years later to take on the remodeling of their farmhouse in Illinois, and as he surmounted the ladder that leaned against Livvy Faraday's inn in Maine, his very muscles seemed to hold the memory of the last work he had done of this sort, the work he had done on his own home. The feel of the hammer hard against his palm remembered and the arches of his feet on the rounded rungs, the tautness along the length of his spine. He remembered working with Nancy.

The two of them had painted the clapboard siding a pale yellow and accented the windows in sky blue. He repaired and refinished the hardwood floors. The roof had leaked like a straw hat in the beginning, and he had put in a few weeks, sweating, swearing, and hammering new shingles over the old. He moved a barn swallow's nest out from under the eaves and fixed the leaky plumbing in the guest bathroom before Nancy's parents came to visit. Renovating the farmhouse was an effort that went on for almost a year and drained their savings account until it was as dry as the old well behind the barn.

As long as Jackson had been able to do the work, they had been able to save money, even if sometimes it felt as though they were spending it faster than it came in. To have called in a contractor would have been admitting defeat. Jackson could work outside all summer, while he patched, sanded, and painted inside all winter. When Nancy was pregnant with Nathan that second summer, she complained guiltily about not being able to help more. She talked to her belly at bedtime and said that as soon as the baby was born, he better be ready to go to work helping his dad.

Now, with the brisk sea breeze blowing over him, Jackson stood on the ladder propped against the high eaves of the inn, listening to the sounds up high in the trees and remembering the hours they had put into their house. Why did some things stay so clearly with him, so vividly? There was a moment, a summer moment when he looked down and saw Nancy lying on a quilt in the yard, languorous with the child inside her and the buzzing prairie heat. The shadow of the house bisected her: her face was in the sunshine, her hair bright. From the shoulders down, though, the shade lay on her like a blanket. He had stood and looked at her for a long minute. It was such an odd sight from his high angle, his wife so little down there, cleaved by dark and light, so vulnerable. It had been strangely touching.

Their house was standing empty now, his and Nancy's, though he could feel it in his fingertips here on the slate roof, though he could feel it in the ache of his left calf, holding his weight. And he knew that for the rest of his life anytime he stood on a ladder, he would recall how he had stood so high above that red clay earth with the sun in his eyes and a paintbrush in his cramped hand as Nancy opened her eyes and held her hands to her eyes against that burning light and called up to him from the ground.

"Hey, how's it going up there?" Livvy called.

Surprise surged through him. He hadn't heard the car in the drive or her footsteps on the stone walkway through the garden. Reflexively he wrapped his hands tight around the rungs of the ladder to keep his balance. "Not bad," he said.

"Am I going to need a new roof?"

Jackson slithered down the sides of the ladder like a kid. "Nope, but there's some trouble."

She was smiling at him, the directness of last night restored to her manner. Her eyes didn't bounce off him as they had this morning. She stood with her hands on her hips. A pose, he thought, the way she thought people should stand when they were surveying work to be done. She was so earnest in her ways. "Must have been that bad ice storm in January," she said. "It knocked the top of that maple down."

"That would do it."

"George came out with his chain saw and cut it into firewood. He nearly broke his leg doing that job, too."

Jackson leaned against the house, surprised at how hot it had been up there, how dazzled his eyes were, how dizzy he felt. The sun was high in the sky now, mounting toward the warm solstice and away from the dark. He leaned into the shade of the eaves, his hand resting on a windowsill. The paint was riven with cracks. He ran his fingertips over it. "This trim wouldn't object to a fresh coat of paint," Jackson said.

"George was going to do that before he got laid up," she said, shrugging as her eyes scanned the height of her inn. She was standing several feet away from him, just beyond the shadow of the house. She was wearing a white blouse that bared her arms.

Hers was a tiny frame, Jackson thought. Whatever she was shouldering because of her husband was an emotional feat of strength, not a physical one. She was fragile, like women in old paintings. Her bones were not what one noticed about her, nor was she wound together with the muscles of athleticism. Hers didn't have the definition of Nancy's body, those lithe strong arms and hard legs. It was Livvy's flesh that attracted, its very pinkness and softness, its freshness. Livvy was almost antique in her beauty. There was something old-fashioned about the way she lived in her body, so gently. All her gestures were graceful and unhurried, yet purposeful. Altogether, her outward appearance was most about who it was who lived inside.

Who lived inside?

She caught him staring.

He looked away.

"You must be thirsty."

He nodded.

"Come inside then." He followed her. She poured him a glass of iced tea, and they sat on the porch together, watching the ocean, content to let the sound of the waves do their talking.

Livvy insisted on helping. He had her steady the ladder (although he didn't think she could bring much to bear against his weight and that of the ladder, against gravity itself). And she handed up supplies while he worked. She stood on the ground in her work clothes, which were faded overalls and a white cotton tank that scooped low under the arms so that he could see the barest swell of her breasts, a pearliness. It made him aware of his eyes, keeping them away from those armholes, the thought of that opalescent skin. He remembered how soft her fingers had been the night before, so warm and dry. He couldn't forget.

Now she wore a pair of thick leather gloves.

Jackson made himself concentrate. His first job was to slip a hacksaw blade underneath the slate to cut through the old nails. Then he'd be able to remove each damaged piece of gray slate. He placed the slate pieces in a bucket he had carried up for that purpose. Once the broken pieces were removed and the roofing felt was tacked back in place, he measured the sizes he would need to cut. He scurried down the ladder holding on with one hand and carrying the heavy bucket in the other. Maybe he was moving with too much confidence, maybe he was thinking about her watching him, but a few rungs before the ground, he grabbed for the ladder and instead got a handful of air. It wasn't very far to fall, perhaps three or four feet, but it ambushed him.

"Jackson!" Livvy said, trying to break his fall.

He landed on his back on the grass, gasping astonishment. She was beside him, knocked over too.

"Are you all right?" he said. He lifted his head, checking that everything was still connected to her as it should be, to him. She was exclaiming concern. But when she saw that his back wasn't broken and that there were no compound fractures, she began to laugh. "What happened? I've never seen anything like that."

"I don't know. Maybe I can do it over in slow motion."

"No!" She giggled. She rolled over and laid one of those soft hands on his chest. "I don't want you breaking your neck trying to fix my roof."

Jackson began to sit up. "It just proves that gravity still works, I guess."

"Well, I wish you'd find another way of proving it." A strand of Livvy's brown hair, scented with a light perfume, brushed past his nose. He could see strands of gold in it up this close, and the copper also. She turned to him, and her laughter subsided, her expression softened. She leaned in to him, looked into his eyes, then closed her own. She brushed her lips against his.

His breathing stopped, or else he had never regained his air from the fall. And she too gasped as they pulled apart, all in one motion. "I'm sorry," she blurted.

He drew a breath. "It's all right." He laid a finger along her cheek, stroked the outline of her face. She was white with the realization of what she had done.

She brought her hands to her face, buried it. "I didn't mean . . ." she said. She pulled away from Jackson and tried to get on her feet. He reached for her hand and held it tight. As he watched, brightness spread up her neck and into her cheeks.

"I said it was fine." He could see that she was panicked and ready to bolt. And really, he was too. He was embarrassed and ashamed and confused. He was filled with a sense of having betrayed someone—himself, or her, or was it Nancy? Or all three of them?

But that kiss was just a moment, he told himself. It was gone now, vanished into the past, receding already. It had happened and it was over. Just like everything else. It was over. "Don't," he told her.

Still, she tried to pull herself up, away.

He couldn't let her go. There had been something else too.

Warmth. A sensation of security, of belonging. There had been something found in him, rediscovered however fleetingly. He couldn't completely let it go. "Don't."

She stopped struggling. But he kept his fingers curled around the narrow stem of her wrist, securing her.

"I just don't know what I'm doing sometimes,"she said. "I'm just churning with emotions. Maybe I'm going just a little bit nuts. Who wouldn't? I've been feeling pent up for so long and when you arrived with the cooking and the help with the inn . . . Sorry."

"It's been good," Jackson said. "Doing these few things for you, it reminds me of who I used to be."

"But . . ." She looked up at the sky in astonishment, then swung the gaze to him. "I'm married, Jackson."

"No one knows what goes on inside a marriage," he said. "But you're having a rough time, and you're alone. Naturally you're feeling emotional. Who wouldn't?"

He held her wrist because she let him. No matter her words, she seemed to welcome it. The cool blades of grass brushed his ankles, and he heard the hum of a truck passing on the road in front of the house. His back felt stiff, and he eased his weight up against the trunk of an oak a few feet away and pulled her along next to him. He could hear her breath faintly. He hadn't realized how much he had missed feeling the warmth that came off another person.

She spoke in a voice that was unlike her, flattened and thin.

No music, only frailty and hurt: "It took me a long time to even say the word. I still feel like I can't."

He nodded, not following her meaning yet, but wanting to encourage her.

"Howard always worried about me because he was older," she said. "But I expected that we would have more time together. He was the one who used to kid around, calling himself my first husband."

"Was it a stroke?" Jackson asked. "Is that why you're alone here?"

"In a way I wish it had been, then maybe there would be some progress or something. It's worse." She lapsed into silence, stared toward a stand of cedars lining the drive.

He spoke, only to fill in the absence of her words, only to keep the door open between them. "It must be difficult for you, running the inn and both your lives."

"Taking care of this place is sometimes the only thing that keeps me sane," she said. "Of course, I wanted to keep him at home as long as possible, but how could I?"

He nodded. He understood the strange, almost unconscious, guilt one feels at being the sole survivor of a family. It's a feeling of wanting disaster to take you all at once.

"Howard required extraordinary care," she said. "He walked in on people in the shower. Or he sat down at tables and ate someone's breakfast. Or chased guests out when he couldn't figure out who they were. As much of a nightmare as it was for me, it must have been far worse for him not to be able to make sense of the world around him."

"When did you first notice he was having trouble?"

"It's hard to tell," she said. "I remember about four years ago, just after we had finished the renovations. Howard was hanging some pictures in the lobby, and he couldn't figure out how to hold the hammer. It was the strangest thing. He would tap on the wall with the wrong end, or turn the hammer around and hold it by the head. He just couldn't figure it out. That's when we both started to worry."

Even as she revealed the details of her husband's Alzheimer's disease, Livvy kept her emotions at arm's length, ducking from their blows like a boxer. Sometimes she laughed about what she told him, like the trouble she had getting her husband to put his shoes on the right feet. He would dress in a business suit and jam his right foot into the left wing tip and his left foot into the right shoe.

"There was no way to get him to put them on right," she said. "He could be as stubborn to me as he had once been sweet." After that she banished all his difficult-to-wear clothes to the attic and replaced them with running suits and Velcro sneakers.

There was no medication that had worked, she told Jackson. They had tried every promising lead. A friend had sent her vitamins and liquids with multisyllabic names, encased in gel capsules, but those didn't do anything either.

"And then he hit a guest," Livvy said. "A poor, overweight, very pale English guest." There was nothing that sparked the argument, only that the guest had brushed shoulders with Howard on his way in for breakfast. "Howard has no control over his temper," she said. "He just drew his fist back and let it fly into the Englishman's gut.

"Did they sue?" Jackson asked.

"No, people are pretty understanding if you're honest with them. They left me flowers when they checked out, and the name of a doctor in England who was doing research. I sat on the edge of the bed and cried, just that simple kindness. And also, that's when I knew I had to move him somewhere." She flinched at the memory. "I had help here, but it was too much to handle. Luckily, I got him a room in the home here in town. It's small, a good place where I can visit comfortably. A nurse I'm close to calls me when he's agitated, and it helps if I go see him for a while. He knows my face even if he doesn't remember my name every time he sees me. These last few days he's been troubled." She sighed.

Jackson nodded. "I'm sorry," he said. "I wish I could say more than that. But there isn't anything more, is there?"

She turned and looked at him deeply. "See, that's what is getting me in trouble. I know you know. There are no words. There is no science. No answer. No rescue. You know that."

He looked at his hand where it held her wrist. A blue vein ran under his finger, and he pressed against it, felt her pulse.

She sighed. "Living like this really clouds my thinking."

Jackson nodded. He knew how grief exploded in your head like a grenade, and threw shrapnel of anger, fear, and heartbreak into every thought. He remembered how reason meant nothing, how he lived for the chance to hunt down the reckless drunk who had killed his family. Confessing his desires had only inflamed them, and when it was over he felt nothing and ran. *Until now,* he thought.

Just then a pine green pickup truck with a caved-in driver's-side door pulled into the drive. The woman behind the wheel turned slowly and pulled onto the lawn as Livvy scrambled to her feet, embarrassed at having been caught this way. She brushed hard at the grass clinging to her overalls and walked toward the truck. Jackson got up and followed. A man with a round face, tanned by cigarette smoke and the Maine winter winds, leaned out the passenger window and studied Jackson. "Are you the man with the exploding truck?" he asked.

"I guess I am," Jackson answered, chuckling to defuse any tension.

"Jackson," Livvy said. "This is the guy who saves my life at least once a week. This is George. And his wife Mary."

Jackson nodded to both. George took his hand in an iron grip. "Just wanted to see who this character was," George said. "Can't be all bad if he's patching your roof for you."

"He's not bad at all," Livvy said.

Mary nodded her approval.

"No, I guess not," George said. He finally released Jackson's hand.

"How's the leg, George?" Livvy asked.

"Slows me down when I chase Mary around the kitchen," he said, with a wink.

Mary shook her head.

George looked long and hard up toward the roof. "That's not the way I would've done it, that's for sure," he said. "I hope that slate holds through the winter. Sure enough I'll be up there myself come the next bad storm."

Mary nodded.

"Jackson's doing a fine job," Livvy said, trying her best.

George shrugged. "At least he won't be running out on the job from what Sammy at the garage tells me."

"No, if I go anywhere, it'll be on foot," Jackson agreed.

Mary's mouth formed a tight pucker, and she shook her head.

"Well, I'll be back at work in six weeks, the doctor says. Less if I have any say about it," George said, staking his prior claim.

"There'll be plenty for you to do," Livvy assured him. "Howard always said the place could keep a staff of ten employed."

They waved as Mary started the truck and began to back down the driveway. She ground the gears when she popped it out of reverse in the street, but hunted around and finally got the old truck to move forward.

"Does his wife ever speak?" Jackson said.

"Only when she answers the phone for him," she said, and a laugh tumbled from her. "I've never heard her say a word beyond hello."

"I guess that broken leg isn't going to slow him down all that much," Jackson said.

"It should keep him off ladders for a while." Livvy looked over at him, sliding her eyes in a cautious way.

"Sorry to have put you in a dicey position." He acknowledged her manner as he nodded toward the trunk of the tree where they had been propped together.

"He'll have the whole town talking about you—more than they already are," she said.

"It wouldn't be the first time," Jackson said sadly. "I'm getting used to it by now."

They shared weak smiles at this irony and stood side by side in the tall grass marred by tire prints. Jackson's eyes rested on those impressions, such simple things, two parallel lines pressed in the lawn. But there wasn't a thing—simple as tire tracks or complicated as the stirrings of love—that could ever happen again that wouldn't remind him of Nancy spotting Nathan as he balanced his bike the day the training wheels came off, or of Franny waving her little yellow cap as she rode the neighbors' Saint Bernard like a pony. There wasn't anything that wouldn't somehow remind him of what he had lost, and how. And standing here with Livvy now, he was aware also of a warning, something deep within him that said he was vulnerable to loss even yet.

Chapter 8

The course of nature . . .
seems delighted with transmutations.
SIR ISAAC NEWTON (1642–1727)

Jackson showered, scrubbing the spots of dried latex paint from his skin, as if he were peeling away the layers to his core. He had finished repairing and repainting the patch of water-damaged ceiling upstairs. Showers were a good place to let loose, and he knew well how to let the water run over his face as he howled like an animal into the spray. It had become a ritual that gave him a momentary release for his rage. But something happened this time, some connection was completed, and when he turned off the shower he began to cry. His tears came suddenly, flooding his cheeks. His knees buckled, and he collapsed on the tiled shower floor, and he lay there, with his legs pulled up against his chest. He had not cried like this since it happened. All these months his sadness had twisted and throbbed inside him, trapped beneath the temper he had inherited from his father.

In a while he recovered himself, though he still felt raw. He stepped out of the shower and wrapped himself in the thick terry robe hanging on a bathroom hook. He sat on the bed in his room with a towel around his neck, trying to regain control of his emotions. His photo albums were stacked on the small desk next to a china vase lamp. Steeling himself, he ran his fingers over the colored vinyl covers and bravely flipped open the cover of the album on top. On the first plastic-covered page, there was a picture of Nancy by a mountain stream in the Blue Ridge Mountains. He looked away from the photograph as he recalled the scene. They had taken their first vacation together against the backdrop of those mountains in the fall. They had driven an impossibly long distance just to be alone and away from their work.

They had stayed at a quiet bed-and-breakfast run by a Mennonite family and had made premarital love every which way in the antique sleigh bed in their room. They ate at tiny cafés that smelled of fried potatoes and biscuits. And went to the movies in a mall they didn't know, but it didn't matter since the mall looked the same as the one at home. Following the Blue Ridge Parkway, they toured the Great Smoky Mountains, lost in a velvety cloud of love.

They stopped to hike at a trail that led through the forest. Jackson slipped a small pack over his shoulders to carry the camera and a few snacks. They hadn't walked more than fifteen minutes before they came to a cool stream that tumbled over moss-covered stones. Nancy floated a leaf in the water and watched it travel with the current. She cooled her hands in the stream and touched them to her face.

"I want to vulcanize with this," she said.

"Vulcanize?" he said. "Are you going into the rubber business?"

"I just want to be part of everything here," she said, pressing on. "You, me, the leaves, and this stream. It's like I want to be able to tumble apart into my most basic molecules and mingle with everything for just a moment and then come back together again. Then I would know what it was like to be the water, the air, and you." She wrapped herself around him. "I want to be inside your skin."

He had kissed her forehead and felt the cool droplets of water on his lips. Then he let his lips move to caress her neck, and brush against her ears. Finally, he brought his lips against hers and they kissed hungrily. They moved off the trail to a rise cushioned with mossy earth and a bed of pine needles. She lay astride his body and moved her hips against him. In a moment they were one.

She had taught him how to love her. It was all a matter of

timing, they had found. They learned from each other, and they had found a rhythm that was right. But time had tricked them and it ran out on their lives quicker than either one of them had ever expected.

He took a deep breath and flipped the pages in the photo album. Nancy had arranged all the pictures and there weren't nearly enough of her because she was always the one behind the camera.

She had a face gentle with soft curves and lips that turned upwards in a coquettish smile, and the Kodak color image was all he would ever have to remind him. He flipped the pages past pictures of Nancy and Jackson alone and together, past the shots of their small family wedding at a friend's summer house on the South Jersey shore, and he paused for a long while at a photo of him leaning over to kiss his son's soft skin. The memories pulsed in Jackson's brain, but they didn't make him want to cry or rage until he felt like tearing his head off his shoulders. These pages of light-exposed paper were like recalling a dream he had once had.

Jackson had been on the roof the day they were taken from him. He had been installing an electronic weather station so he and Nathan could monitor the winds and temperature above the trees. He mounted the windspeed indicator and the electronic temperature sensors on one end of the high gabled roof. He would run the wiring inside to a console where they could read off the weather's vital statistics. Jackson was going to teach Nathan how to watch the dips in barometric pressure and rise in relative humidity so they could predict summer thunderstorms. They could graph their results and then compare them to actual storms and at the end of the season they would have a good idea of their accuracy.

He remembered how Nancy had hovered nervously as he worked, afraid, as she always said, that she would hear the thud of his body falling off the ladder into the lilac. Jackson wasn't happy about being up there either, his arms aching and the muscles in his legs jumping like sewing machine needles. He balanced carefully on the ladder and secured the instruments with heavy bolts and then drilled a hole in the siding to pass the wires down through the attic wall.

"Will you promise to stay on the ground while I'm gone?" she had asked him before she left. She rolled down the window of the car, and he leaned his head inside and kissed her again.

"No ladders," he said. "Hurry back."

He had waved to Nathan and to Franny, strapped in her car seat, and then watched as the car drove down the long gravel drive, past the front yard that was wide enough to grow a few rows of corn. He didn't know then that they would never come back. It was such a warm Saturday, still early, before the temperature rose enough to wilt the herb garden. He snapped open a bottle of iced tea, swigged it too fast and gave himself a stomachache.

When he had finished pulling the wires through the interior wall, he mounted the console and powered up the weather station for a test run. The dials spun and the green diodes glowed with numbers. Wind was blowing gently from the southwest at eight miles per hour and the pressure was holding steady. Nathan would be delighted with all the buttons to push and the numbers they could record. He was young, but had just enough of the curious scientist in him, and Jackson wanted to encourage it.

At lunchtime, Jackson grilled himself a Swiss cheese sandwich in a skillet on top of the stove, and waited for his family to return to him as though they were riding waves into the shore. When the sun began to stretch low in the sky, the first twinges of worry bit into him, so he punched on the TV and watched an inning of baseball for distraction. He drank a beer and as time passed his fear circled like a shark, moving in ever tighter circles.

Einstein said that all observations are relative to the perspective of the individual. And while the perception of the passage of time remains the same for an astronaut in a rocket accelerating near the speed of light, to observers on the ground, the clock on the spaceship's console would appear to be slowing down. This was a phenomenon know as time dilation, and Jackson felt it hard. He watched the wall clock in the kitchen. Its hands throbbed like a heartbeat, but never seemed to move forward. He thought about calling someone, a friend, or the police. It was as if the rest of the world had suddenly surged forward at near light speed, leaving him behind, suspended in a jellied weightless vacuum. The sun still worked its swing shift with the moon, but for Jackson, time held its choking breath.

When the police car pulled slowly up into his driveway, he

knew. As the uniformed officer took steps up the stone walkway to ring the bell and make his notification, Jackson closed his eyes tightly. He knew that linear momentum was the tendency of a moving body to continue in motion along a straight line. He could see in his head the parallel black rubber tire tracks that shot wide across the four lanes of Rangeline Drive in front of the Republic Bank like an experiment in motion gone terribly wrong. And he knew that momentum was a vector quantity, and therefore moved in the direction of the body in motion. All three bodies. He could see them trapped in the wreckage of twisted steel. He knew they were gone.

The next sound he remembered hearing was the thump of the Sunday paper landing heavily at the front door of the farmhouse. He had never been alone for long in that house, and sound seemed so much louder when he was surrounded by the silence of the dead. In the blue light of the early morning, he dropped to his knees on the lawn to read the headlines, black and reflectiveless as the killer's eyes in the color picture above the fold. Jackson let out a small cry. The police were calling the accident a vehicular homicide on the grounds that the man behind the wheel of the pickup truck that jumped the center line at seventy-five miles per hour and landed flat on Jackson's family was drunk.

Jackson writhed on the ground, digging his fingers into the earth. He let the paper fly from his hands and scatter above the lawn, like doves released into the air. Wal-Mart advertising, coupon supplements, comics, *Parade*, and the Home section went flapping across the yard. He crawled inside the house, and the silence detonated in his ears like a sonic shock wave.

The answering machine groaned as it rewound the yards of tape beeping and squealing. He had ignored the phone that had rung and rung all night long. On the machine were messages from reporters at the newspaper and TV station. There were halting condolences from colleagues at the university or friends who had sat stunned through the late news. People wept, they called out to him for reason, and they cried for explanation. There were no interpretations Jackson had to offer. It was only another series of a billion random actions and reactions occurring in the universe at that moment in time. Only it had happened to him.

But he hadn't expected the aftershocks: the temblor of journalists and camera crews as they pounced on the yawning chasm of his grief in the aching moments afterward, even before Nancy, Nathan, and Franny were lowered into the hot clay earth. At the funeral, three days later, the mourners tripped and threaded their way through the long tails of coaxial cable leading from the remote trucks. His family's story had gathered a frenzied momentum and the local news anchor pleaded with Jackson to do sit-down interviews where the camera could lovingly pan over his family's pictures displayed in silver frames on the living room coffee table. Did they expect Jackson, who had suffered so greatly, to explain this high-velocity collision of mass with a few choice adjectives?

He talked with the city press in the front yard, but he didn't invite them in the house. And they twisted this into something vaguely suspicious, and wildly eccentric. It was simply that his grief felt so private. Jackson's sketches of the children and Nancy hung on the walls in the house. He had conjured their likenesses from black lines on paper, scratching the pen across the page. And Nancy's photographs were displayed in frames of antique silver or folk-art painted wood. He didn't want the family photographs punched up to materialize in the upper right corner behind every TV announcer in the state. He wanted the privacy to grieve over his family, secluded in the house where he could still feel their presence.

In the dim light at the end of his first day without them, he suddenly felt enraged. It overtook him like a speeding car, possessing his body and rolling through his veins like nitroglycerin. He swept an arm across the kitchen counter and cleared a row of glasses to the floor. It seemed that he heard them crash to the Mexican tiled floor before he saw the shards of glass explode. He wanted to drop to the floor and roll across those pieces, feeling them carve into his skin like knives. The impact of the glasses had chipped the soft clay tiles that he could have pulled up with his fingernails, chewing through the sandy grout with his teeth. He wanted to find that drunk and split his gut wide open with a dagger of glass. He wanted to feel the man's blood wash over his hands. His desperation was nearly uncontrollable.

There was much to arrange, between planning the funeral and consoling relatives on the phone. His grief would have incapacitated him, but his anger served him well, propelling him through his tasks. It simmered just below the surface and broke loose like a rabid animal when he was alone.

"What's all this?" Reverend Fitzhume said on his visit that day. Michael Fitzhume had made himself indispensable to Jackson, handling the press, making phone calls and arrangements. The sandy-haired priest had come and gone all through the day, while Jackson was coming apart.

Jackson had been alone and pulled out a shelf of books and let them spill across the floor. He had drop-kicked several heavy titles to the opposite wall. "I just don't understand," he told the priest.

"No one can make sense of this, Jackson," Fitzhume said. The Catholic priest had been hardened on the streets of Chicago, ministering to the city's poorest and running a shelter in the most threatening neighborhoods. He had been robbed at gun- or knife-point twenty-seven times and was proud of it. Taking a job on the campus of the university at Wendell in the quiet farmland two and a half hours south of Chicago was his stab at early retirement.

"Jackson, let the police handle it," Fitzhume said. "They'll bring you the answers you need."

"I don't need answers!" Jackson yelled. "I need them back."

Fitzhume laid a hand on his shoulder. "I know," he said. His voice broke, and he steadied himself. Then he stooped his short, round body to the floor to help Jackson pick up the books he had knocked over.

But Jackson couldn't wait patiently while the police investigated. He went in search of answers, fueled by anger and the black coffee he had lived on for the second day straight. He wanted to gather information, and though he knew that his first stop should be the scene of the crash, he drove back roads to avoid it. He didn't know if he could ever stand to see the stretch of road between the mall and the movie theaters where they died.

The police offered to come to him, but Jackson insisted on going to the station house himself. He worried that it was the streak of denial that ran in all the Tates, that somehow it was an affirmation of the tragedy to have a detective sitting on the couch where he and Nancy had watched movies and shared a Coke with ice and lemon after the kids were in bed. But Jackson saw himself too clearly to slip into the somnambulism of his parents after an emotional shock. He bristled like the array of antennas in the desert sweeping the cosmos for a faint radio signal from a distant intelligence. He wanted to be totally immersed in the police investigation of the crash.

There were two detectives assigned to the case and all they could offer him were apologies and condolences. He sat with them at their desks as they explained that there was a suspect and they had statements from witnesses, but they had no answers for Jackson. Then they led him out. They had nothing for him.

Jackson paced through the station house, looking for the suspect, the man he had seen in the newspapers and on the news. He remembered the tangled greasy dark hair that hung around his balding head like a beaded fringe curtain. He searched for him in the lineup room with the one-way glass. There was no sign of him at the sergeant's desk, where the new suspects were fingerprinted and photographed. And down in the basement lockup, he couldn't find him either.

"Jackson," his friend Levi Bloom called to him on his way out to the parking lot. He was slightly built with a neat, ginger-colored beard and long light-brown hair that strayed over his round wire glasses. He was dressed in a blue shirt with a wildly colored tie, which he said his wife had bought him from the collection designed by Jerry Garcia. "Kate and I drove over last night to check on you. We've been leaving messages . . ."

"Sorry," Jackson said. "I've been spending all my time with Fitzhume going over things."

"Yeah, I know," he said, focusing his eyes intently on the oily sheen of the new asphalt covering the police station parking lot. When he looked up at Jackson, he seemed wounded, on the verge of tears. "What happened was a shock to all of us. Nancy was a good friend to Kate. She's just devastated, and me, I can hardly believe it."

"Thanks," Jackson said, feeling detached. He laid a hand on Levi's shoulder and squeezed. What more could he say? All day, Jackson had been consoling the friends who were trying to console him. At the dry cleaners when he brought in his suit, he soothed a long line of customers with trembling lips and averted, moist eyes. In the bank, where he had a check certified for the funeral home, the bank manager broke down in her office, and

Jackson offered the comfort of his shoulder for her to cry on. They had all read about the accident in the paper, seen the footage of the crash scene on the TV news, and some of them had even left flowers and tiny stuffed animals at the scene. Maybe this is what drove his tears away and fueled the anger in his chest. Nancy, his only comfort, was gone.

"They probably didn't tell you, but the judge has set the arraignment for tomorrow morning," Levi said, sighing hard.

"The funeral's tomorrow," Jackson said.

"It's better this way," Levi said. "At least the judge thinks so. You came here looking for him, didn't you?"

"Yes," he said. "But they wouldn't tell me anything."

"Could we go somewhere and talk?" Levi said. His voice had a reedy quality that lent an earnestness to everything he said.

They drove to a roadside picnic area in a strip of green by a murky creek on the outside of town. Jackson followed, tailing Levi's old Subaru wagon with the VISUALIZE WHIRLED PEAS and SPLIT WOOD, NOT ATOMS bumper stickers. Some time ago, Jackson and Levi had fallen into an easy friendship. Their wives were best friends at work and made the plans for all of them. Their kids were even about the same age. In the winter, they had gathered at the snow-covered hilly mound in Wendell park, christened it Suicide Mountain, and all loaded onto a pink plastic toboggan to ride all the way down. They grilled veggie burgers for the vegetarian Bloom family on the Fourth of July and gorged on homemade vanilla custard ice cream. Levi had a reputation as the city's most unorthodox lawyer, and he taught a class at the law school on working pro bono and lawyering for the indigent. He made no apologies for wanting to be the William Kunstler of the Midwest. But the Chicago Seven and radical agitators didn't need defending in near-rural middle America. Levi made his living preparing wills, arguing dog bite cases, and working the occasional trespassing trial. As luck would have it, the trial of the century in Wendell was Levi Bloom's own trial for possession of scarcely an ounce of marijuana. He risked playing the fool and argued his own case, winning an acquittal on a technicality. Business had slowed for him ever since.

They sat down at a picnic table heavily carved with initials and four-letter words. Levi wrestled with a broken latch on his battered leather briefcase and shuffled some papers around.

"Juice box?" he said, offering him a drink. "Kate buys them for the kids' lunch, but I always snag a couple."

Jackson let Levi place one of the paper containers in front of him. "What did you bring me out here for, Levi?"

"We gotta talk," he said. "I know everything's still fresh, but I think you have to act quickly here." He sipped his juice. "Jackson, you need someone out there for you. Richard Polk has a good lawyer, and he's going to use all his tricks to get this guy off."

"What's your point, Levi?" Jackson said. "I've been getting calls from lawyers since the night it happened. If I park in town, they cram business cards under my windshield." Jackson stood up from the picnic table. "I'm burying my family tomorrow, and my mind is not on filing a lawsuit."

"Look, the D.A.'s colon is tied in a square knot, and the judge is trying to do the right thing, but you need more. The truth is you need someone out there representing you, digging up dirt, talking to the press. Everyone wants to see Richard Polk go to jail for a long time."

He could hardly bear the sting of the name of his family's killer on his ears. "What can we do?" Jackson said. He seethed, all he wanted was to see Polk dead in some medieval fashion—stoned, stabbed with sharpened sticks, boiled in oil.

"Once the trial gets under way, I want to bring a civil case against Polk. Basically, Jackson, I want to be out there stoking the fire for you. There's a jury pool out there now, and it's never too early to start your opening argument. Influence them from the beginning, let them feel your pain."

"If you could talk to the press for me . . . that's all I need. No fireworks. Just answer their questions. I can't find the energy to face them," Jackson said. He wrapped his hand over his forehead. "I don't know what they want from me. Why don't they bother him?"

"They figure you'll crack easier," Levi said. "A man grieving over his family makes for good footage. So from now on, let me take care of them, and I'll start looking into filing for wrongful death damages."

"It's not about the money," Jackson said, feeling the words spring from somewhere deep in his gut. "He shouldn't be walking the earth after what he did to my family."

"You don't have to tell me that, Jackson. Besides, a jury has about as much sympathy for a drunk as they do for a child molester. But I know you have expenses. Polk owns a business. He should be paying."

Jackson had been writing checks for the funeral arrangements all morning.

"We're sick over what you're going through," Levi said. "Just sick." He seemed to want to reach for Jackson and offer him some kind of comfort. He pushed his wire rim glasses off the bridge of his nose and massaged his eyes. "Let me do something for you. This is what I became a lawyer for."

"God knows I need to do something," he said. "What else is there now?" Already he was daunted by the prospect of ever returning to his everyday life of teaching and coming home early on Friday afternoons. His life had ended with theirs, and he didn't know how to begin to make another one for himself.

"Take it easy," Levi said. "You're in deep shock now. We all are. Just let me be your ears and eyes out there."

Jackson agreed, but he wasn't hopeful about anything. How could he be? All his hope had vanished, replaced by a nebulous, noxious cloud that choked out the life inside him. Theories come and go, the atmosphere of a distant planet might be determined to be ammonia one week and chlorine gas the next. Whether it is a confounding of the instruments or the senses, no one knows. But he knew how quickly rumors about the canals on Mars are quenched by data from unmanned probes only to be replaced by *Enquirer* stories about Elvis's face sprouting like a pimple on the red planet's surface. Reality is too slippery a concept to grasp, coated with some kind of superslick friction-reducing compound cooked up in the DuPont lab. Jackson didn't know how to hold on to it. Instead he let it spin into flux, metamorphosing into human fear, not hope.

When Livvy knocked on his door, he was lying with his face buried in the down of his pillow with nothing but the shrinking purple light of dusk illuminating his room. He felt dizzy and a feverish sweat dampened his hair against his face. She knocked again.

"Jackson," she called. "Are you okay?"

He could never be okay again, of course, but it was a question asked of him so often he no longer offered an answer of any thoughtfulness.

"Are you hungry?" she said, revising her query to something he could genuinely respond to. She understood firsthand the meaninglessness of her question. He felt sure she had heard those same questions from those around her, and had come to realize, as had Jackson, how absurd it was that one should be expected to coherently express grief. Livvy continued, her voice hesitant, alert that she might be disturbing some moment of sorrow. "I made you a sandwich for supper."

Jackson found his way to the door and opened it, squinting into the lighted hallway. "Sorry, I was just lying down." He smoothed his hair.

She stood in the doorway holding a tray with a turkey sandwich and an iced tea. He invited her in and then, realizing his room was dark, he stumbled toward the nightstand to turn on a lamp. On the bed were his open photo albums. Nancy, Nathan, and Franny looked out at him, smiling, lovely, alive.

"I thought you might be hungry," she said. He caught her looking at the photos with a quick glance as she walked toward the desk. He flipped the covers closed and put them away while she set the tray down. "I can't believe how much you got done today. You must be exhausted."

"Pretty near to it," he said. "I took a shower and passed out cold after that." He didn't tell her about how he lay there and sobbed, and how positively lost he felt. He realized he was still wearing a bathrobe and pulled it tight around him.

"Thank you," she said, moving toward him. "I knew I needed some help with things, but sometimes you don't realize how bad you need it."

"You needed it all right. I have a list as long as my left leg of things to do tomorrow." He was attempting a joke. But it wasn't coming off.

"Don't overdo it. This place could keep you busy for years," she said, laughing to fill the long pause afterward. She bit her lip awkwardly. "Look, I'm sorry about what happened out there when you were working on the roof."

"Please . . ." He held up a hand to stop her. Jackson wasn't about to indulge her regret over a kiss. He didn't have that much strength left. His emotions felt as though they were gathering toward a critical mass. He felt unstable enough that he might just melt down. He wanted her to stop. He didn't want to overanalyze what had happened, or banish it from memory, or deride it. It had happened. For better or worse, she had made him feel again, and deeply: He felt his loss, his terrible, bone-penetrating loss, and worst of all, the beginnings of hope. He was torn between these, shredded by his own feelings, their conflict. How could he go on; how could he not?

"We're both strung out," he said. "I mean, you with your husband's disease and me—I don't know. What we're going through short-circuits us. That's how I feel, anyway."

"I know, but until now, I've been able to deal with everything myself," she said. "I don't usually take anything lightly in my life."

"You shouldn't," Jackson said. He sighed.

She studied him, then pulled him into the circle of light cast by the lamp. He resisted. But she could see now. She could see the red in his eyes, the sorrow there. "Jackson," she whispered, running her palm along the upper stretch of his arm, just that.

"Will you stay with me while I eat?" he asked, motioning toward a chair.

She nodded.

He sat down himself and ate the sandwich. He didn't feel an obligation to talk, and in a sense, he trusted her because of her willingness to endure his silences. She was content to sit with him. Recognizing this about her, feeling gratitude, a surge within struck him like an unexpected wave. Tears ran down his face and fell into his plate. Still, she waited. And it was just what he needed.

Chapter 9

*The total mass of the products of a chemical reaction is
always the same as the total mass of the original materials.*
LAW OF CONSERVATION OF MASS

That night Jackson dreamed that his sorrow was like smooth river
stones that he polished with his tears. Three stones had turned to
jewels that were embedded in the palm of his hand. Then in his
dream, he saw the skin close over the diamonds in his palm until
there was nothing except the variegated crisscross lines that told
his own story.

He didn't recall the dream until he was talking with the insurance adjuster at Rockpoint Mobil, where the crisp husk of the

Quark was concealed under a blue tarp. Something about the banality of the transaction freed his mind to wander. He thought of Livvy back at the inn, stripping the dusty cobwebs of winter away in time for the weekend when the first guests were scheduled. She had made him feel something: His own torment, yes. But more.

"If you'll just sign here, Mr. Tate, I'll take a few Polaroids for the file," Bromley, the adjuster, said. He was a slight, perspiring man. He swabbed at his damp forehead with a plaid handkerchief.

Jackson accepted the clipboard of forms from him and signed in triplicate. Bromley took pictures from three angles and laid them on the hood of his car to develop.

"Do you think you could take one picture for me?" Jackson asked. "Sort of a remembrance."

"One wouldn't hurt." He lifted the camera to his eye. Jackson shifted. "No, it was better before you posed," Bromley suggested. "Just stand naturally next to the car."

Jackson moved back to stand in the angle of the open side door. He could still smell the acrid odor of burnt plastic. He thought of how odd Livvy would think it that he was being photographed with what might have been their death trap. Although he knew it would have appealed to Nancy's dark humor. She would have laughed if she had a picture of him with the remains.

"That's it," Bromley said, squeezing the shutter. The Polaroid pumped out the photo, and he held it in his hand as the image materialized from behind the clear chemical screen.

Jackson found his favorite sketchbook under the backseat of the Quark. It had escaped the fire, though the edges were flecked with the dried foam used to smoother the flames. He flipped through the few charcoal drawings he had made in the spiral-bound book of the house and a doodle he had done of a pirate for Nathan. The pirate had a patch over one eye and wore a cloth wrapped around his head. He had drawn this character for his son to give him something to distract him enough so Nathan would play on his own and let Jackson finish a pile of work he had brought home. Instead, Nathan had tricked him into spending time with him. Jackson had pushed aside his laptop computer and his data graphs to reach for a sketchbook. Nathan worked a marker on a piece of drawing paper and copied his father's sketch. Entertaining his son before bedtime was something no father could resist.

There was something in that sketch that lured another memory out of Jackson. He remembered when he was Nathan's age, riding the train back out to the green suburban lawns with his father, leaving the film-noir grime of midtown Manhattan. A foursome of men had the side of a cardboard box propped on their laps, dealing poker. Their cigar and cigarette smoke fogged the air between the tailored wool suits and wing-tip shoes. He recalled his own father skimming a number two pencil across a scrap of paper set on his own briefcase. He had sketched a pirate, bandage on his cheek, parrot on his shoulder, and it was good. Jackson was six years old, riding in the seat next to him, listening to the bright tenor of the conductor calling out the next stop, and he was thrilled.

"I always had a talent for drawing," his father had told him. He showed Jackson how to shape the drawing, tracing ovals for the head, body, arms, and legs, then refining, adding details, building the image. "But you can't support a family doing silly drawings."

In his father's desk drawer, which smelled of newly sharpened pencils, Jackson discovered the sketch and his own childish copy. His father had been dead a week when his mother had asked him to look for the insurance papers. David Tate had kept the bundle of paper in his desk drawer, close to the things that mattered— last year's tax return, a ledger of household expenses, and the set of silver Cross pens with the ancient tool emblem of the Masonic Lodge that had belonged to his own father.

What is it that parents cherish from their children? When the homework was done and the bedtime battle had ended in a draw, Jackson could have sat listening to the steady rise and fall of Nathan and Franny's breath through the night. How he loved the sweetness of their breath. It reminded him of the delicate honey of the air on a spring morning. He got used to Nathan's shrill cry of pleasure at chocolate pudding after dinner. He agreed to read Franny *Green Eggs and Ham* one more time. His and Nancy's sleep-deprived first year was worth it when Nathan made a cooing gurgle that might have, maybe, almost sounded like "Da-da." Then, the explosion of firsts, as he grew into a boy who made his own decisions, and pursued his curiosity in the world in a way that reminded Jackson of himself.

At eight years old, Jackson had glued together complicated models, including warships of the British navy and a McDonnell Douglas DC-3 from the 1930s. He had no interest in play unless it involved acquiring a new skill, whether that meant completing a model of advancing complexity or devising a method to inject a bead of glue into a tight spot under a wing. By his ninth birthday he had saved enough from his allowance to buy a cheap soldering iron. This allowed Jackson to work on electronics projects, building radio sets or simple burglar alarms that he could set up to go off if someone (like his mother) came into his room.

"At least disconnect that thing when you're at school so I can get in there and clean," she told him.

"Mom, that's the whole point of a burglar alarm," he told her. "To keep people out."

"Fine, mister," she said. "You can be responsible for cleaning up your own mess."

That was fine by Jackson. He wasn't hiding anything illicit, not comic books or bags of Double Bubble he had lifted from the newsstand, like friends did. He had a dozen experiments and projects in partial stages of completion. Entering into his room required the care of a tightrope walker to navigate around the net of wires and transistors.

Jackson built equipment to order, too. Once his older cousin,

Freddy, wanted to have his own interview show like Johnny Carson. Freddy, a teenager with his hair pomaded into a slick blond pompadour and a collection of velvet smoking jackets, asked Jackson for help. And Jackson went to work, constructing a device that would do what Freddy wanted. After Thanksgiving dinner, Jackson unveiled his black box device to Freddy, who took it up to his room. His desk and an adjacent couch were angled to face the door, just like the *Tonight Show* set. The family indulged Freddy in his hobby and were always willing victims to be interviewed as he adjusted his prop microphones for each guest. With the right mix, it could be a gas, as Freddy coaxed Aunt Midge and Uncle Philip into revealing some nugget of their courtship as the reel-to-reel tape recorder rolled. Freddy needed the practice, but with the black box Jackson had designed, he could take his show to a larger audience.

It was nothing but a miniature transmitter that was set to interrupt on the same frequency that NBC radio broadcast on. There wasn't enough power to jam the radios in more than the immediate neighborhood, but the impact would be tremendous. Freddy would be taking his show out of his bedroom and into the living rooms of most of the houses on Lily Drive. He chose his guests carefully: Jackson's mother, Freddy's older brother, Marty, who was home from college, and Harry Burns, who once thought he had developed a limp, until he knocked the pebble out of his shoe.

Jackson tuned in the radio in his aunt and uncle's living room in time to hear Freddy sound out the three-note chimes of NBC on a toy xylophone. He welcomed his guests and offered up a commercial endorsement of his favorite, Orange Crush soda. Jackson's father was the first to notice.

"Hey, is that Freddy on the radio?"

"Yeah," someone said. "What the hell is Freddy doing on the radio?"

The phone rang as Freddy asked his cousin Marty how many girls he had kissed in college. Someone was calling to say that Freddy was on the radio. What was this? Did NBC give him his own show?

"No, of course not," Freddy's father shouted into the phone. "We don't know how he got on the radio. He was just here eating a piece of pie and then all of a sudden, he's on the radio."

He wasn't on long. A capacitor overheated on Jackson's transmitter and before Freddy could ask Jackson's mother when she had first kissed his father or if Harry Burns had ever kissed anyone at all, the regularly scheduled top-forty hits programming was returned to WNBC with a pop, a crack, and a puff of blue smoke.

It was those happy things from his own childhood that Jackson thought about, and then the realization stabbed him that his son would never have his own triumphs. Nathan would never know what it was like to outsmart a roomful of your relatives or build a device that could alter the airwaves for even a few minutes.

His grief was all about what wouldn't be. About what Nathan and Franny would never have, never do, never feel. All Jackson's memories felt tainted, and one by one they all succumbed to the noxious, hardened steel reality that his children, so full of possibilities in their burgeoning awareness and in their particular personalities and in the strength of their own little fingers, were dead. Nathan would never find this pirate drawing in his dad's belongings and think of the bedtime they had drawn together and of the story Jackson had told him of his own childhood, of his own father's pirate sketch. The future was halted in the past.

"The police didn't find tire skid marks to match to Polk's truck," Levi Bloom had come over to tell him the night before the funeral. Jackson had been pacing slowly from the kitchen to the living room and back again. The beer he was holding by the neck of the bottle had grown warm.

"I don't know what that's supposed to mean," Jackson said. He surely did, but he couldn't force his thoughts in that direction.

Levi touched Jackson's shoulder, and they both stood still. "It means he was so drunk, he didn't even bother to hit the brakes."

Jackson wrenched away from his friend and walked on into the kitchen. He dumped his beer into the sink. With his back to Levi, he beat his fist against his heart so hard that he felt it jump in his chest.

Jackson made his own way back to the inn from town. He decided to leave Livvy to attend her work, and he sat in the cool breeze of the yard under the gnarled maple. He faced the inn, opened the sketchbook he had recovered, and with quick strokes of charcoal on paper, began to sketch the outlines of the house.

In a while, as he was filling in the detail of the decorative porch brackets, Livvy pushed open one of the large double-hung windows facing the lawn and began digging in a window box set there. She churned the potting soil, mixing in a few scoops of compost she had brought up from the black plastic tumbler near the back door of the kitchen. Finally, when she was satisfied the soil was prepared, she planted pansies in different shades of iridescent copper and purple. Her hands were so tender in their work, as though she were tending a child.

Jackson began work on a clean page in his book, sketching Livvy from his hidden vantage point on the front corner of the property. He worked the narrow bit of charcoal, held expertly in his fingertips, drawing the fine arc of her jaw. He rendered her slender neck, the delicate ovals of her eyes, and the faint pout of her lips. She was concentrating on the flowers she planted, making certain that they stood straight and secure in the window boxes. With a few strokes he captured the tiny worry lines in the knotted skin above her nose. It was clear that even the few moments she had to herself were suffused with a tumult of thoughts. She set down her gardening tools on the edge of the window box and stripped off her canvas gloves. He was still sketching her, impulsively, when he saw that her face was damp. She wiped the tears away from her eyes with her palms. Jackson stood up, letting his sketchpad fall to the grass. She looked at him.

"I haven't cried about it in such a long time," she said, from the opened window. "Now I can't seem to stop."

That was the way it was. Grieving was as mysterious a process as falling in love. Somewhere, deep inside the brain, grief and love were wedded and wound serpentine around each other. Wasn't there a component of grief in loving someone? Implicit in the emotional contract between two people is that someday it will end: One will grieve for the other. Jackson doubted whether love could demand the same urgent attentions of the heart if men and women did not feel their mortality in the shadows of every escaping day. We want so much for love to sweep us away into undying arms, forever. To last for eternity, to last long after bodies have turned to dust in rosewood caskets. We read *Romeo and Juliet* to take some comfort in believing that the lovers died so that they could finally be together in peace, left alone by a world that wanted to pinch their love out like a candle flame. But where and how could they be together?

Heaven, as Jackson imagined it, was no place for lovers. It was cold, India ink black, pinpricked by starlight, machine-gunned by cosmic debris, and pierced by comets hurtling through the void by the violent tug of opposing gravitational forces. As a fervent believer in the scientific method, he saw no evidence to the contrary: The life we are each living at the moment is, most likely, all we ever get.

Maybe, he thought, that is why those in love feel a pain that walks hand in hand with them. Because it is inevitable that someday they must say good-bye. Born alone, dying alone, we do what we can to make the time between not so solitary.

"I've been saying good-bye for years now," Livvy was saying. He was standing under the window now, looking up at her. Her delicate skin was blotched with her emotions. Her eyes seemed more green under the spikes of wet lashes. "I'm not sure I know who he is anymore."

Jackson waited for her to gather the right words. She searched over his head, as if she could find them in the garden that ran to the rock fence, or beyond that, in the reaches of the blue moving sea or at the far horizon.

"There are glimmers of him," she said. "They're like shadows in the background. Maybe he'll say something in a certain way that seems very familiar. And in his good moments, when he's sort of with it, I almost expect that he'll turn to me and say, 'Livvy, get me the hell out of here.' "

"It's cruel."

"It is," she said, sighing gently. "I know nothing can be done. Hope can be a curse, sometimes."

They both heard the car in the drive at the same moment and they turned, she in the window, he on the ground. She said, "I better see who's here."

Whatever musings Jackson had about the quiet country life of an innkeeper were quickly dispelled by a few of Livvy's battle stories. She had told him tales of guests who behaved as though paying for a night in the Rockpoint Inn entitled them to be waited on as though they were royalty. Or the guests who couldn't get enough towels. Or enough hot water. Or enough blueberry muffins. But there were, of course, other guests who had become friends and returned year after year.

Jackson found Livvy in the lobby where she was speaking to a dark-haired man in his twenties wearing a worn denim shirt over his slouched shoulders. His hair was mussed and hung in casual curls around his face. His complexion was pale and had a slick puffiness, like an overripe piece of cheese. Below his jawline was a row of dark hairs on his neck where he had missed shaving.

"Jackson," Livvy said. "This is Mitch Faraday, Howard's son." She reached to touch his shoulder and urge him forward, like a nervous backstage mother at her child's Christmas pageant.

Jackson extended a hand to Mitch.

"Hey," Mitch said.

"Jackson's helping me open for the season," Livvy explained. "You remember George? He broke his leg."

Mitch nodded. Shyness seemed to radiate from him like radio interference from sunspot activity. He was a few centimeters taller than Jackson. His eyes darted around as though he were a skittish, shy, burrowing mammal. He seemed grateful when Livvy led him toward the hall and a room at its end. He flipped the strap of his black nylon duffel over his shoulder and followed.

Jackson retreated alone to the bar, where he climbed onto a stool and finished his sketches. He could hear the murmur of their voices, Livvy getting the son settled.

"I guess I never told you I was a stepmother," Livvy said when she appeared. She was edgy and clasped her hands together tightly.

"Seems like a nice enough kid," Jackson said.

"He is. Especially for someone who's been through so much." She went around the back of the bar and reached for two long-stemmed glasses from the rack. She pulled the cork on a bottle and filled two glasses.

"Cheers," she said, raising her glass.

Jackson nodded. He let his eyes follow her quick motions. There was something so birdlike about her suddenly, so flighty. "What is it, Livvy? I've seen physicists calmer in the lab the night before they announce the Nobel prizes."

"I don't know," she said. "Howard's so much worse since Mitch saw him last. It's doesn't seem fair. Mitch has been taking this hard and as much as I want him here, visiting with Howard, I know it's not easy for him."

"My father had a heart attack," Jackson said. "I drove all night to New York to be there. I made it just before he died. He knew I was there and I think it meant something to him, but it wasn't easy."

"Were you glad you saw him?"

"I was relieved, I think, and sad, of course," Jackson said. "But I know how important it is to say good-bye. And I'm sure Mitch knows that, young as he is. It's a long good-bye with Alzheimer's, isn't it?"

He gave her a meaningful look and she returned it, acknowledged the sad truth of his words. She leaned across the bar and touched his arm. "Poor kid."

"He wouldn't be here unless he wanted to be."

"That's true," she said. She sipped at her wine. "Howard was married for twenty-two years before he met me," she said. "When Howard's wife divorced him it was harder on Mitch than anyone. He drifted from one prep school to another. But somehow he made it through college."

"There's not a term paper or a final exam that you didn't help me with," Mitch said, gratefully. He stepped into the room. He seemed more relaxed now, though he still didn't look directly at Jackson.

"I knew how much your father worried about you." Livvy mopped a wet spot off the counter with a rag. Mitch shifted awkwardly in his black canvas hightops.

"She tutored me long-distance for my French class," Mitch told Jackson.

"I tried," Livvy said, as she laughed. "Mitch would fax me a copy of the lessons and we'd go over it and over it."

"I flunked anyway," Mitch said. He sat down next to Jackson at the bar. "*C'est la vie, n'est-ce pas?*"

"*C'est vrai, mon ami,*" Livvy said.

"Lost me there," he said, grinning.

"How about something to drink?" she asked him.

"A beer, please." Mitch stepped up to the bar. Livvy opened a cold beer and set it in front of him. He wrapped his hand around the long neck and brought the bottle to his lips.

"How's work?" Livvy asked.

"My editor says I couldn't meet a deadline if I was writing my own obituary."

"What kind of writing do you do?" Jackson asked.

"I've been writing for an alternative magazine in L.A.," he said. "It's a start, you know. I've been on the road with this band, writing an insider's story on touring. Anyway, we're just sort of idling in Boston before a summer tour. So I borrowed a car and drove up. Just kind of spontaneous, you know. I was basically here before I knew it." He drummed a thumb nervously on the counter and took a quick swallow from his drink.

"Glad you came," Livvy said.

"Yeah," he said. "But I should have called first and given you some warning."

"Are you kidding?" Livvy said. "If I had known you were as close as Boston, I would've come down to get you myself."

Mitch pressed his tight lips into a smile and began to peel the label back on the bottle with his thumbnail. "How's Dad?"

"He asks for you," she said.

"I wish I could have been here more," Mitch said.

"If there's one thing he would understand, it's that you were working," Livvy said.

"Talking about work," he said. "I better check in before the long weekend."

"You can use the phone behind the desk, if you want," Livvy said, as he walked into the lobby.

"He likes you," Jackson told Livvy after Howard's son had left the room.

"We try," she said. "We both love Howard after all. But Mitch has his own life."

For the first time, she looked over at Jackson's sketchbook, lying opened on the bar and saw her face. She looked hard at the black lines and white space that made up her features. "You did this?"

"When you were working at your window boxes," Jackson said.

"I look tired," she said.

"Then I got it right." He smiled at her, teasing.

She clucked her tongue.

"It's genuine, wearing your experiences in your expression."

"Yes," she said. "I've always thought it was sad when people tried to change their looks, when they had a face-lift, or an eye-lift, tried to erase the wrinkles. Like they were something to be ashamed of. I remember the first time I noticed wrinkles at the corners of my eyes, I was so startled. I stood in front of the mirror and made all these faces, happy, sad, mad, to try to see where I had got them. And it was laughter," she said. "They came from laughing. And I figured I had earned them with a lot of happy moments. They belonged to me."

He laughed.

"So now when I look and see how I've changed these last couple of years, I think there's something right about that too, something beautiful. I'm losing my husband. Why shouldn't that show in my face?"

"You are beautiful," he said, holding her eyes with his.

She kept his gaze for a moment, then defused the gravity of the moment by saying, "But a scientist who sketches? Isn't that some sort of sacrilege?"

"It's just something I do when I feel like it, that's all. My dad used to draw to keep me quiet on the train or on car trips." Jackson had taken his father's talent, passed on to him by blood, and had used it for science first. He had begun as a teenager, he explained to Livvy, sketching visual references in the margins of his chemistry and physics notes. It was a way to understand the complexities of molecular bonds and the vagaries of gravitational theories. In college, he kept an unlined book for his drawings, going first to them to understand the expansion of space and time. Visualization was the physicist's most difficult task, and seeing the results of lengthy calculations illustrated on paper made them real. At times, understanding the movement of the universe seemed beyond the abilities of the human imagination, until they were revealed by pencil and paper. Drawing made Jackson feel like Leonardo da Vinci, sketching his outlandish designs for flying machines and sixteenth-century machine guns. An imagination is a scientist's greatest tool.

That would have been it, art enslaved to science. If it hadn't been for Nancy. He had sketched her at her insistence. The results were stiff. He had posed her so formally that she looked only like a distant cousin to herself. After a while, though, Jackson had found his own loose style, self-taught and simple. It worked well enough to render the images of those close to him. It freed his mind from the constraints of logic, and he learned to love the release, knowing intuitively that this dabbling helped him "see" the physical universe with more clarity. And it had entertained the kids in a way that his labwork certainly never could.

For Livvy, he placed the charcoal on the paper now and began to work it back and forth. She watched his fingers move as he coaxed her image from the smooth white page. His movements were quick, his eyes darting from her face to his own hand, moving, flowing, moving. And soon her image began to emerge out of the blank space, the face Jackson thought suited for a cameo pin, so classical in its smooth beauty, the abiding sorrow only lending her a look of resolve and calm and dignity. When he looked up at her the last time, her eyes were shining.

Chapter 10

*It is impossible to determine both the exact position
and exact momentum of a body at the same time.*
THE UNCERTAINTY PRINCIPLE

Jackson lay spread-eagled on his belly to tighten the small screws holding the bottom length of a wobbly porch railing in place. He turned the screwdriver hard and felt the blunt handle wearing a blister into his palm. It had been years since he had worked this hard.

He rolled over and sat up, leaning back against the house. There was one project after another on this old inn, and he just kept finding them, as if he needed to find them. Once he discovered a problem, he couldn't let it be, leave Livvy alone with it. And after a winter's neglect, even the small jobs had grown exponentially. Loose screws had worked themselves nearly out of their holes, leaks had materialized out of nowhere, creeping rot had resumed under a sagging section of gutter, and paint had curled like hair on a humid summer day.

Mitch stepped out on the porch and lit a cigarette. He looked over at Jackson after he'd taken a long drag. He pulled the cigarette guiltily from his mouth. "I'm down to three a day," he said. "Besides, Livvy doesn't like me to smoke in the house."

"Tough habit to quit," Jackson said. "Chemistry works against you."

"I sort of have this theory that if I taper off enough, maybe one day I'll just forget to smoke, and I will have quit without even knowing it." He took another drag. "Probably not, huh?"

"I don't think I could fool myself like that."

Mitch nodded and looked out at the view. "Where'd she go?"

"She's out hunting for dinner."

"I wish she wouldn't go through so much trouble," Mitch said.

"She wanted to do something special." Jackson dropped his screwdriver back into the toolbox.

"She always does," he said.

Jackson finished his job and loaded the toolbox. "Well, I guess I'll drag these tools back into the garage." He stood up and slipped past Mitch on the steps.

"You know," Mitch said, quietly. "Livvy was the happiest person I knew."

"Was she?"

"Sometimes I thought I'd go crazy from how much she laughed. She would get on a roll, and watch out. And my dad, he'd just tweak and tweak, egg her on. Those two."

"I knew someone like that once," Jackson said.

"Funny how life can just stomp that right out of you." Mitch rubbed out the butt of his cigarette, grinding it hard with the toe of his sneaker.

Jackson nodded hard at Mitch, in agreement and in good-bye, and feeling the lump rise in his throat, he turned and walked toward the garage. At least the kid was learning early enough to harden himself a little against life's shocks. Jackson himself had just been broadsided. The laughter, the happiness had seemed a guard against harm, a barrier. He had known better. He had known the laws of the universe. He just hadn't believed they applied to him, not when he would come home from the lab and find his wife and two kids puddled on the bathroom floor, collapsed in laughter. Happy beyond all belief.

Sometimes, scientific examination exhausted Jackson. There was a point at which details blurred to the eye and fuzzed the brain. It was possible to be too focused and see only data streaming out of the beautiful Milky Way, viscous with the swirl of distant solar systems. And there wasn't a scientist around who didn't need to step back from the microscope after a while and refocus on something outside the cold agar of a culture dish. Jackson still marveled at human imagination, able to wrap its neurons around ideas that had no more substance than air, but he hadn't yet found his balancing point. Where the eyes were blind, algorithms and calculation gave sight. The darkness of superstition had been beaten back with the laser beam of science. He knew it was practically heresy for a scientist to think so, but sometimes he wondered if there wasn't a certain peace to not knowing. This drive to seek, know, and understand, where was it leading us? What was it leading us away from? But maybe, he thought, we needn't have gone so far to learn so little. For while we were learning, we were also forgetting.

It wasn't only Livvy's Howard who had introduced Jackson to that disease of forgetting. He had seen it at work in a colleague at the university. An economics professor with a terrific squash game suddenly couldn't figure out how to play. And it struck another professor's wife, stealing away the recognition of her children, and forcing her husband to retire early to care for her. Outside the stratosphere of Jackson's cloistered university family, he knew there were many other victims of the disease, circling their own neighborhoods in a white heat search for their own homes, or ruining a favorite recipe for cherry pie with a cup of salt instead of sugar. Jackson had seen how it dismantled people neuron by neuron.

He set the toolbox back on the workbench in the cool darkness of the garage. There were some old wooden hand tools in a crate under the table. Jackson picked up a molding plane and held it in his hand. The handle was darkened and smoothed by years of use. There were other antique tools for shaping and finishing wood. He found a scrap board and peeled a long ribbon from it with the plane. The blades needed sharpening, the tool had tugged and bucked in his hand, but someone had cared for these once. Years ago, a carpenter wasn't reliant on electricity or engineering ingenuity to use these tools, he simply had to practice. He had to work at it until the tool moved expertly in his hands, so he might turn out objects of grace.

Jackson looked out at the inn through the wide-open frame of the double garage doors. It could not have been easy to keep all those guests happy while Livvy watched Howard lose more of himself every day. She had to attend cheerfully to her guests on their vacations no matter what was happening. It was an acting feat, and Jackson had done it himself. As enormous as his grief for his family had been, and as privately as he had wished to mourn, he still had to attend to the guests who had arrived at the funeral. He remembered how the three caskets of diminishing size had sat next to the open graves at Mount Hope Cemetery. It was searingly hot as the funeral party stood at the treeless plot on the burnt brown grass. There had been so little time to think about decisions that should have been made over the course of a lifetime.

After it happened, he went alone to the mortuary, where he chose those caskets as the lanky funeral director, his lips pursed sourly, offered somber advice. "You want to think of them always in comfort," Mr. Olsen had told Jackson.

And so Jackson examined them as though he were appraising a new car. Olsen encouraged him to touch the lavender satin, and feel the delicate plush comfort. And the wood made a difference too, he was told. A hardwood withstood the deteriorating elements of the earth better than soft pine. And a top-of-the-line copper casket stood up better than any other. In fact, Olsen guaranteed the copper to be tight for one hundred years. Olsen pointed out the superior brass hinges and the deeply padded sidewalls of the hardwood models. And of course, the finish was superior, with ten coats of hand-polished lacquer to protect it. Jackson spent the children's college fund. He and Nancy had so carefully accumulated it by depositing a hundred dollars every month at the university credit union.

The massive marble stone he bought would have the family name carved in it, along with the names and dates of the two children and his wife. It would fit flush with the ground, as were the new requirements, so the groundskeepers could mow around it easily. Jackson's information would be chiseled in place when his time came, although standing under the cloth awning at the burial listening to it snap in the wind, he wanted to lie right down with them and feel the anchoring weight of the dirt shoveled over him.

There had been a visitation that morning, followed by a service at the university chapel, in which no one, not even Reverend Fitzhume, could overcome sorrow to speak. The three caskets sat on wheeled stands before the preacher, his hair as white as the petals on the lilies and his face a shade of bright red only a fair-skinned Irishman could achieve. He managed only a handful of words before his voice broke. He bit down hard on his lip and turned to the Bible for words of calming inspiration.

"God teaches us . . ." Fitzhume began before he faltered again. He gazed out upon the eyes of the congregation until his blue eyes locked with Jackson's. His face crumbled like an ancient artifact dug too roughly from the earth. He stepped back from the pulpit and signaled the organist to play. After the first bar of "Nearer, My God, to Thee," he turned away to gain some control. Jackson watched his shoulders quake and felt embarrassed for the man who had been such a good friend to his family. Fitzhume and Nancy had worked together raising money to restore the stained-glass windows in the university chapel. They had been constructed by a partner of the famous Louis Comfort Tiffany. But now Nancy would never see the completed job that would restore their splendid colors. And neither would the children the priest had come to know after long working dinners at the house, where Fitzhume and Nancy stayed at the table long after the coffee had grown cold, plotting and planning.

Jackson and Nancy weren't Catholic and they weren't even particularly religious, but Jackson wanted no one other than their friend presiding over the service. Fitzhume must have thought that he could hold his grief at a distance and maintain his equilibrium, but it was those quenched emotions that surged forward as he stood before the bodies of a family he cared for. Finally, after an interminable pause, Fitzhume climbed to the pulpit once again. "This is a tragedy from which we may never recover" was all he could say to conclude the service.

Hired limousines followed Olsen's hearses. A police escort had been arranged to lead the motorcade out to the cemetery. The chain of cars wound slowly out to the state highway, headlights blazing and the police lights spinning silently. Jackson sat in the backseat of the limo traveling behind the hearse with Reverend Fitzhume at his side. Fitzhume was holding his hand and patting it gently.

"I'm so sorry," he whispered. His head was bowed. "That's never happened to me before. I've ruined it all. I'm so sorry, from the bottom of my heart, Jackson."

"Don't . . ." Jackson said. His voice sounded strange and unearthly to his ears.

"But it's my job to comfort the grieving," he said. "To tell you they've gone to a better place."

"My understanding of the universe and its rigid laws doesn't allow much room for a God who rewards and punishes," Jackson said. "I don't much believe in a better place."

Reverend Fitzhume sat up slowly, as he composed his thoughts. "What was it you always told me?" he asked. "What

Einstein said?"

Jackson sighed. "He said, 'Science without religion is lame, religion without science is blind.' "

"Find a way to make sense of this, Jackson. Whether it's through God or Einstein."

Fitzhume's face relaxed into the calm of the quiet epiphany. He blotted his nose with a graying cotton handkerchief.

Jackson watched the new shopping centers near the mall and fast food restaurants tick past the window. They paused at a light, a policeman held back the cross traffic. They passed a crumbling fragment of curb, ribboned with a single set of rubber skid marks. There was the fire-streaked wall of the bank where the stucco had been crumbled by the high-speed impact of the vehicles. Fitzhume let out a wail of sympathy. "My god! Couldn't they have taken us another way?" the Reverend said, waving his hands in the air.

Jackson's eyes locked onto the sight. He knew there had been no way around without looping five miles out to the interstate, but he hadn't been prepared to see where his family had been abandoned to the cruel laws of motion. By the time the limousine turned into the gates of Mount Hope, past the gateway's inscription of "forever in heaven," he was weeping.

Chapter 11

*An important scientific innovation rarely makes its way by
gradually winning over and converting its opponents. . . .
What does happen is that its opponents gradually die
out and that the growing generation is familiarized
with the idea from the beginning.*

MAX PLANCK (1858–1947)

Jackson wrestled with the lobster on his plate until he thought he
was going to have to go hungry. He had wrenched off the head
from the body, following Livvy's lead, but that was about as far as
he could get on his own. Instead he concentrated intently on the
cole slaw.

"Should we let him starve or help him?" Livvy asked Mitch. They were sitting in the yard at a picnic table built of planks of rough-hewn hemlock. The weather had turned decidedly toward summer, swerved really. It was balmy and they couldn't stand to go inside. The sunset sparkled on the ocean and tinted everything the color of the melted butter in the tiny cup by his plate.

"Better give the guy some pointers," Mitch said. He split open a huge red claw with a pair of lobster crackers.

"Hey, it's been a while since I've worked on one of these," Jackson said. "Have pity on a guy."

"I'll give you one lesson, and a lobster will never give you any trouble again," Livvy said.

"Watch her," Mitch warned. "She can dismantle one of these things like I've never seen. The lobster just sort of steps out of its shell, like out of a winter coat."

"Okay, show me what to do," Jackson said.

"Well, you've already got the head off, that's a start." Livvy picked the lobster up off her plate. "Follow along."

"Here I go," he said, picking up the body of his lobster.

She snapped off the claws and set them aside. Then she broke off the tailfins and pushed the tail meat out in one piece with her finger. Jackson grimaced and did the same.

"You have to get down and dirty with them," Mitch said. "We can hose you off later."

"Okay, now start working on the claws." Livvy delved in after the tender meat in the claws. "Now dip it in a little butter like this, squirt it with lemon, and feed yourself."

"That's it?" Jackson asked with his mouth full. "The meat tastes like the sea itself."

"You can work on the little legs, too," Mitch said, sucking on a leg between his teeth.

"There's something very carnivorous about this experience," Jackson said, waving a claw. "All the carapace-cracking, picking apart, and dissecting."

"Don't go any further with that, professor," Livvy said. "The only thing that gets you through eating a lobster is not paying one bit of attention to what you're actually doing."

"Never look at the green stuff in the head," Mitch said.

"No kidding." Jackson lifted up the head to look and grimaced.

Livvy had baked an apple cobbler for desert. It was rich enough, but she added a scoop of vanilla ice cream to each serving. The three of them sat back with their bowls and their sticky fingers wrapped around their spoons and watched the night overcome the day in a calming display of every shade of purple.

Later, when Livvy was washing the dishes and Jackson was drying with a soft dish towel, he heard Mitch's car slip down the driveway. Jackson watched from the kitchen window.

"Sort of late for a beer run," Jackson said.

"He's going over to see his dad. He's been working himself up to it all day," Livvy said. She drained the water from the sink and tied up the trash bag containing the lobster remains. "He says it's easier when he goes at night. It's quieter."

Livvy served breakfast the next morning to a couple from Albany who had checked in for the weekend. And she went on to catch up on some chores. Jackson began work painting the trim on the front of the house. He dragged the ladder around from the garage and spread a cloth out. Livvy dragged a rug outside and shook it out over the front porch railing.

"You really don't have to do all this, Jackson," she said.

"It's no trouble." Jackson opened a gallon can of paint with a screwdriver and stirred it. "You can't let this stuff go. It'll only look worse."

"If George wasn't out of commission . . ." she said. "All I'm doing is working you," she said.

"I can take it," Jackson said. "Besides, I have to do something to justify my stay, right?"

"Jackson," she said, and carried the rug inside.

Even the way that word sounded on her tongue was enough to make him want to stay. Jackson. His name. Like a couple of notes of music, a lullaby, such comfort.

He should have left days ago, that much he knew. He would have been better off if he had just packed up after one night of rest. Livvy knew enough of his story, and what was left, he hadn't dared breathe to a soul. He should have been far away from her when the Quark burned, and he could have waited for his insurance check in some roadside motel with a mildewed shower curtain and cigarette burns on the bedside table. That's where he really belonged, chasing the guilt of what he'd done around his mind like a dog chasing its tail. Instead, he was with Livvy, in consolation and conversation: distracted from his own sins.

It was more, though. He felt it, tried to ignore it. But it was there in simple reminders, like the way she called his name. She exerted some hold on him, pulling him toward some place of happiness. He had recovered something the last few days with her, and it was like finding a pirate's treasure buried on the beach. But he wasn't ready to make sense of why he stayed with her, if only to allow that he wasn't as alone. There had been a dozen cities over twenty thousand miles where Jackson could have lost himself in a crowd.

Jackson dabbed his brush with paint and began with the trim of the windows that faced out on the porch. He worked with deliberate, practiced strokes, applying the paint evenly. When he finished, he raised the ladder up carefully against the shingles on the side of the house and climbed. He began with the second floor corner windows, working carefully with a small brush to do a neat job. After a while, he stepped down the ladder to move on to the next window.

There was something meaningful to him about this simple work. Maybe, had he lived in another time he would have become a member of the Society of Shakers, and lived out his life as a widower with work as his worship. He could have devoted his days to building nesting wood boxes with hand tools.

Maybe the work soothed him so because it made him recall his own house, and the care that he and Nancy had devoted to it. He had loved making it theirs with nothing more than paint and putty and hard work. Never had he felt so right as he had in that old farmhouse. The blue slate sink in the laundry room with the brass faucets, the rectangle of stained glass that cast colored sunlight on the hardwood stairs. But that sense of being home had vanished with his family.

He had ended up sealing the house like the tomb it had become. Now he thought of it like an Egyptian pyramid standing out on the prairie. The closets were filled with bright garments. Bottles of spices lined shelves in the kitchen. Colorful children's toys wasted on pillows. Some adventurous archaeologist like Howard Carter, who excavated King Tut's tomb in the 1920s and is said to have died from its curse, might arrive centuries from now and sift through that house in the cornfield. But Jackson had left no curse on the house. Instead, he felt as though the curse, if there was one, traveled with him.

Neither Levi Bloom nor Reverend Fitzhume knew where he had gone. Levi had made a call to Jackson's mother in the week after his friend disappeared just to make sure he wasn't "dead in a ditch." That was exactly the ironic phrase Levi had used over the phone, and it had upset his mother. Jackson had spoken to her from a booth in a truck stop, to offer reassurance and say he was coming to see her. It troubled him, that message she relayed, since he didn't understand if Levi was trying to tip him that he knew and that the police knew too. Levi's particular phrase described exactly what Jackson was guilty of.

If Levi Bloom did know what Jackson had done, then probably everyone in Wendell did too. After getting Levi's message, Jackson had driven without stopping to rest for the night. Gradually, though, he steadied himself enough to relax and weave a loopy, meandering path that led to his mother in Florida. He was alert for roadblocks and cruisers with their lights flashing red and blue. His heart stopped if they passed him on the road in pursuit of other criminals.

Jackson heard voices below him on the porch. His ladder was propped against the back edge of the inn, concealed by a bushy hemlock. It wasn't his intention to eavesdrop. He was only painting the trim outside an upstairs lace-curtained window. Perhaps they thought he had gone into the garage for another bucket of paint, but he could clearly hear Mitch in heated conversation with Livvy.

"Just listen to me for a second," Mitch said.

"Okay, okay," Livvy said. Her voice was strained with impatience and irritation.

"I remember the first time I saw you with my father. You were coming to pick me up at my mother's apartment and I watched you from the window coming through the parking lot."

"Was that when we went to the Bulls game?" Livvy asked.

"Nope," Mitch said. "We were going to a play downtown, I remember it exactly. But you and Dad were laughing and he had his arm around you. And I don't think I'd ever seen my dad so happy."

"We always had a good time together," Livvy said.

"After everything he went through when my mom left him," Mitch said. "You know, he seemed all right with you."

"We never talked much about your mother," she said.

"You're lucky," he said, with a quick laugh. "But when I saw you with him, I thought, you know, I could be a real jerk about this. I could get all pissy that my dad is with a woman that isn't my mom. I knew I could screw it up for him if I wanted."

"If you and I hadn't gotten along, it wouldn't have worked out," she said. "Howard always paid attention to you, to what mattered to you."

"By the time I opened the door that day, I had decided that if my dad was finally happy, it really didn't matter how I felt about it," Mitch said. "I was going to find a way to be happy too."

"Thank you," she said.

"You know, Livvy," Mitch said. "I know Dad would want you to be happy again."

There was a long silence, and Jackson curled his hands tightly around both sides of the aluminum ladder. He was ready to step down to the ground and move to the next window, but couldn't interrupt them. Finally Mitch spoke again.

"I don't want to stick my nose where it doesn't belong," he said to Livvy. "But you've got to move on with your life. Whatever that means for you."

"Mitch . . ." she groaned, as if he couldn't possibly understand her.

"You took care of him when he needed it. Now he's in a good place, well cared for. I know he wouldn't want you to put your life on hold for him."

"Mitch," Livvy said, her voice rising. "I never did for a moment. There's this inn to run."

"You know what I mean."

"Not really," she said, her temper flaring. "But I don't need you to tell me I'm throwing away my life."

"That's not what I was saying," Mitch said.

Jackson heard the screen door slam.

"Fine! I won't bring it up again," he shouted.

Finally, Jackson skittered down the ladder sheepishly. Mitch was sprawled in a chair on the porch, wearing a ratty red bathrobe and white gym socks. He sighed and ran his hands through his hair. Jackson dropped his brush into a can filled with paint thinner.

"Well, that's what I get for opening my mouth before I've had any coffee," Mitch finally said.

"There's a fresh pot inside," he said. "At least it was at seven this morning."

"So you're a comedian, too?"

"Just trying to help." Jackson stepped back onto the ladder.

"Yeah, as you can see that's pretty dangerous around here," Mitch said.

"All you can do is say what you feel," Jackson said. "Sometimes it works and sometimes not." He leaned over and stirred the brush around in the can of thinner. He worked in silence for a minute, then asked, "How was your dad last night?"

Mitch sighed. "All I can say is just shoot me before I forget how to feed myself."

"I can't imagine a crueler disease."

"When I was over there last night, I remembered a time when I was sick at home," Mitch said. "Maybe I was six or seven and had a fever and an earache. It hurt like hell. Anyway, when my dad got home that evening, he came in to check on me. He felt my forehead and tucked the sheets up to my chin, you know, all those nice things. And then he read *Treasure Island* to me. I was sick for three days and every night after work, he'd read more from that book."

"Sounds like he really knew how to be good to you," Jackson said.

"So, you know, last night, I was looking for the bathroom, and I found this library they have there. And *Treasure Island* was on the shelf. So I took it back with me." Mitch stared out at the sky for a long while. "I read to him. I did it because he's sick too, you know.

And even though it's like trying to talk to someone under water, I think he was okay with it."

"I'm sure it meant something to him. I'm sure it did."

Jackson was out of paint, and he was grateful to go out to the garage to open another can. He had no business trying to teach the kid anything about suffering. Maybe the kid had a thing or two to teach him. It was just the old urge in Jackson. Part of him missed explaining things to his students.

He pried off the lid, and his thoughts turned to fluid dynamics and atomic weights. He examined the heavier pigment solids that had settled in the can and the oily base floating on top. He thought of how the volatile compounds in the paint would evaporate as it dried on the windowsills, leaving the pigment to adhere to the wood. There were compounds, too, that determined how quickly or slowly the carrier compounds evaporated and the paint dried. All this was taken under consideration as Sherwin-Williams exterior white was formulated by chemical engineers at the factory.

These were exercises that Jackson put his brain through for no other reason than to convince himself that he understood the world, when he didn't. Besides, reducing common items to the sum of their individual parts was what a physicist did—only on the scale of atoms. He could dissect household appliances as he was talking on the phone and have them repaired before the conversation was over.

Lately, though, he felt spurned by science, abandoned by the reason he once held in such esteem. Maybe, he worried now, his analytical love for the mechanics of the universe was a terrible weakness. In the dark, stony chambers of his heart, he knew how he had used science as a way to hold himself apart from his emotions. There was an anger that he had always felt, deep and primal, that ran through his body like a wildfire. His temper was fueled by the dispassion of his parents. And science had embraced him, wrapped its spindly arms around him, and nursed his curiosity through the years of Cold War spy satellite launchings, nuclear warhead testing, and space shuttles riding piggyback on 747s. He simply had wanted to know how it all worked.

Science wasn't studied for distraction, though. It needed to provide answers. And at the end of the road on the shores of the Atlantic, Jackson began to realize that he wasn't going to find his answers where they once were. There was nothing in the Greek alphabet of physics that would ever help his heart heal. He had once found comfort in Planck's constant or in revving up the university's cyclotron and counting the tau and theta particles. But they offered him no answers when he needed them most.

"Hey," Livvy said, coming up behind him. She laughed sadly. "I just made up beds that hadn't even been slept in. Sometimes, the way the days and nights run together, it makes me feel so brittle, I'm afraid I'll just wash down the drain one morning."

He cocked his head, stared her in the eyes, and smiled. He just couldn't help himself.

"Sorry, maybe that's something I should have kept to myself." She shrugged.

"No," he said. "I just never could figure out a way to describe that feeling. You did it just right."

"Funny how you get to be an expert at describing your own madness."

"No one knows better." Jackson shrugged.

"You should come in and let me get you something to eat," she said, motioning off toward the house.

"After I get this cleaned up," he said. Even after she had gone back into the house, her words rang in his ears. He was no expert at describing his own madness. He had committed an act so brutal the mere thought of it nauseated him. He hadn't even properly grieved for his family. He had raged. And when he sometimes got a flash of himself from the outside, it shamed him. It was beyond science. It was beyond him.

After the graveside service, Jackson had headed for the tinted darkness of his hired limousine, the reporters closing in around him. Reverend Fitzhume was at his side, trying heroically to swat away the microphones as though they were bees. Across the lawn, Jackson could see Levi Bloom hurrying toward him, his pocket cellular phone pressed against his ear. The press cordon tightened.

"Mr. Tate," one blond female reporter shouted. "How do you feel today?"

"How does he feel?" Fitzhume repeated, sounding incredulous at the bald stupidity of the question. "This man has just buried his family. He's shattered and lost and he'll never be right again." Fitzhume shook his head furiously. "That's how he feels."

"And who are you?" another reporter in a trench coat asked. A TV cameraman stood behind him recording the scene, moving in a slow choreography.

"Reverend Michael Fitzhume," he said. "And you can quote me on that. Can't you see Mr. Tate is in no condition to answer questions? None of us are."

Jackson felt strangely lifeless, surrounded by those journalists. It was as though the beat had gone out of his heart, but his body stood upright and the blood somehow still flowed to his brain. He did not feel the breath enter and leave his lungs. Yet he remained completely conscious. He wore sunglasses against the glare of spectators that day, as if those dark lenses provided any shield to his privacy.

"What's your reaction to Polk's plea?" asked a reporter wearing a toupee that had been knocked askew.

"His plea?" Fitzhume answered for Jackson in the same withering tone of voice. "Unless he pleads for forgiveness, I don't want to hear it." He looked at Jackson, who raised his head almost involuntarily, waiting to hear more.

Levi Bloom suddenly broke through the ranks and grabbed Jackson by the arm. He cleared a path and pulled him away. The press turned as a pack and instinctively followed.

"Back off," Levi barked.

"Who does he think he is?" he heard the woman reporter complain.

"That's his lawyer," someone answered.

"Oh," she said. "We can get him later."

The cars were lined up along a curb near a wrought-iron street sign that marked the intersection of Eternal Way and Peaceable Drive. Levi opened the door and ushered him in.

"What's going on?" Jackson said as Levi slipped in beside him.

"It happened this morning," he said. "I just heard from the D.A."

"What?" Jackson demanded. He slipped off his sunglasses and held them in his hands.

"Polk says he's not guilty," he said, trying to cushion the blow he was about to deliver. "He's had no priors so the judge set bail. He's out, Jackson."

"Not guilty?" Jackson said, his jaw falling slack. "But he was there at the scene. The police dragged him from the car. They found an empty bottle of coffee liqueur on the seat next to him."

"He claims he sometimes delivers liquor for his business." Levi shook his head. "I should have seen this coming, Jackson. It's not the usual . . ."

"He's going to get off, isn't he?" he said, turning to Levi. His voice quivered with an anger that squeezed his vocal cords like a python coiled around his throat. "He's going to just walk away from this."

"Don't think like that, Jackson," he said. "We still have a whole trial to go through. One with a lot of evidence against him. And then we'll file our civil suit and gain control of his assets."

"I don't want his assets!" Jackson spat. He suddenly snapped his sunglasses in half and threw the pieces to the floor of the car. "Damn."

When he got home at the end of the day, passing up the gathering Reverend Fitzhume had arranged in the church basement, he found a hand-lettered poster tacked up across the front door. On the stoop were several bouquets of flowers, three cute card-shop teddy bears, and a Barbie doll lying stiff as a corpse. "We'll miss you, Nathan," the banner read in thick red marker. It was filled with the carefully printed names of Nathan's first-grade classmates.

Jackson felt himself sway as he stood on his front steps. For a moment, he thought he might faint. He held his keys in his fist like a knife. Some black anger swelled and crested inside him. He had insisted on returning home alone. He didn't need to be coddled. But at that moment he realized how little he knew himself. With one sudden explosive movement, he brought the key down on the paper sign stretched across the door. He slashed it in two.

Chapter 12

*The normal objective of my thought affords no insight
into the dark places of human will and feeling.*

ALBERT EINSTEIN (1879–1955)

That night, as Jackson was tapping the lids back onto the paint
cans, Livvy reappeared in the glaring yellow light of the garage's
bare bulbs. She looked worried. Her face was gray and set like
hard concrete.

"Could you help me?" she asked.

He grinned out of one side of his mouth and wiped his hands
with a thinner-soaked rag. He had been helping her all day with
only one break for tuna-salad sandwiches.

She smiled weakly in acknowledgment and said, "It's Mitch now."

Jackson discovered the boy sitting in his car with the windows cranked closed. The engine was running, the brake lights blazed, and Mitch sat nearly mummified in the driver's seat. The car's muffler thrummed like a field of spring insects singing throatily together. Jackson rapped on the window, and the simply turned gold band that he never removed from his finger tapped against the glass. Livvy stood on the porch watching.

"Mitch?" Jackson called. He knocked again.

"Yeah?" he finally answered.

"Are you okay?"

"When I get like this, I know it's time to go," Mitch said.

"You want to talk?"

"Done it before," he said. "It doesn't help."

Livvy walked down to the car. Mitch stepped out, letting the engine idle. He leaned up against the hood of the car, slouched into the embrace of his own long arms.

"Sorry, Livvy," he said. "I've got to go."

"I know. It's all right."

They walked back up toward the porch along the squares of slate set in the slippery grass. She slipped an arm around Mitch's shoulder, perhaps to reassure him that she understood his reasons. Mitch went inside to pack his things, while she and Jackson waited on the porch together.

"It's better if I let him go," Livvy said. "Howard's only my husband, but for Mitch . . . it's harder."

When Mitch came back out, they walked him back to the car. He tossed his bag across the seat. Jackson laid his hand on the roof of the late-model Chevy Nova.

"Are you sure you want to leave this late?" Jackson said. "You could start rested in the morn . . ."

Mitch cut him off with a stare that could freeze-dry all the coffee in Colombia. He shook his head. "I can't stay." Then he turned to Livvy. "I guess in some warped way, we're family."

"Not in some warped way," she said. "We are family."

Mitch leaned forward suddenly and wrapped his gangly arms around her. "Sorry, if I shot my mouth off this morning. It's just . . ."

"I know," she whispered into his neck, patting his back. "Take care of yourself. And call me."

He released her and climbed back into his car. He reached out to shake Jackson's hand. "Thanks for trying."

The engine rumbled out of its idle, and Mitch backed the car down the driveway. Livvy waved as he drove off, his taillights reflecting fiery in the evening fog that had rolled in around them. Jackson stood with her until the light was absorbed in the darkness.

"He can drive away," she said softly. "As much as it hurts him, he has to go and get on with his life. That's his job as Howard's son. To carry on. To live his own life."

"And yours?"

She held her arms tightly around herself and shook her head.

Jackson looked at her and knew what laws she was applying to herself. He looked at her and saw himself.

The laws that had always guided him were the unbreakable laws that ruled the physical universe. He knew how his attentions had always gravitated toward the unseen world of subatomic particles. He still felt guilt over the hours he had spent away from his family, running experiments in the lab at the university. There were more nights than he had intended when he arrived home to a sleeping household, his brain swimming with the formulas of quantum mechanics. All for what? For tracing the tiniest excited particle as it leapt like a rabid flea across a photographic plate. He didn't know then how quickly his family would be gone, disappearing into the ether like those rare radioactive particles, decaying in a heartbeat.

Some elements could only survive in the protected vacuum of a lab chamber. It was as though conditions in their world had to be perfect before they would chisel their brilliant light across silver-nitrate-coated plates, to reveal themselves in the lab. He spent months researching and writing articles on how to excite a particular particle just so, in order to demonstrate a point that was lost on more than 99.9 percent of the general population.

He couldn't help reducing things down into their essential elements. He had long taught his students to think about the small intangibles; after all, it was all those tiny particles that made up the whole. Two bodies move across a physical space, their paths intersect, and then they continue in their elliptical orbits. But there was no formula he could devise to plot a course for himself, he had only to trust natural law.

Physicists, except for the humanist Einstein, were not looked upon with favor by many. This thanks to science fiction movies about insects irradiated into the size of trucks, and to the physicist J. Robert Oppenheimer, who was so repulsed by the power of the bomb he had helped create in 1945 that he likened himself to Shiva, the Hindu goddess of destruction. But the average, benign physicist wasn't interested in world ruination, only in measuring subatomic phenomena.

And how does a physicist quantify the roil of emotions in his own heart? Emotions are as much a part of the unseen world as atoms, yet they can't be extracted, centrifuged, or have their particles accelerated through space. Jackson felt as though he was snared in a dizzying algebraic equation, squared and cubed and dazzled to the power of ten. Maybe he'd never calculate an answer.

The world was full of known facts already, a dozen centuries of enlightened guesswork and accidental observations. There were constant forces at work. Water freezes at zero degrees Celsius, boils at one hundred. Light will always travel at 186,000 miles per second, and the lives of those you love must always come to an end.

Livvy sighed in the darkness next to him and then turned toward the house. She took the steps slowly, walking away from him. He listened to the heavy, resigned fall of her tread on the porch steps. Then she appeared as a black silhouette against the yellow light of a window. She looked terribly alone.

Chapter 13

Every particle in the universe attracts every other particle with
a force that is directly proportional to both of their
masses and inversely proportional to the square
of the distance between them.

NEWTON'S LAW OF GRAVITATION

Livvy was too quiet at breakfast, and he was no better. Practically the only thing spoken was his suggestion that they go for a walk. She brightened at his words, and even though they had just eaten three-egg omelets and double helpings of hot muffins, she packed an impromptu picnic in the time it took him to go upstairs and lace up his hikers.

On the south end of the beach was a narrow path that rose up from the sand through the flowering bushes that huddled low against the wind. There, Jackson followed Livvy along the edge of a rocky cliff, following a trail that rounded the point. It bumped uphill, and they had to reach for handholds among the gnarled roots that poked through the earth and footholds among the flat rocks that had been wedged in place as steps. The path was tacked on to the cliffside like the decorative gingerbread molding that trimmed the corners of the great homes they could see rising on the wide plateau above them, where every so often a large gable or turret appeared through the thick growth. Deep shrubs, studded with spring buds, shielded the lawns and gave the summer residents their privacy.

Below Jackson and Livvy, the clear green sea swelled and crashed against the seaweed-covered rock. The waves came in great splashing gusts and then retreated, slowly inching back with the tide and leaving shallow pools in the crevices. Sometimes she stopped and stood looking out over it, sweeping her eyes across the expanse. Then she would turn back to the path, only pausing to point out things she didn't want him to miss.

Once, a cluster of plants grew in the shade of a hemlock that was stunted and tamed by the elements into a natural bonsai. Livvy ran her fingers through the green leaves low to the ground and picked a tiny pale-red berry.

"Teaberry, just a little mushy," Livvy said, holding it out for

Jackson. "Want to taste it? Hardy little thing hung on through the whole winter."

Jackson put the fleshy berry in his mouth and chewed. "Wintergreen?"

"Milder, though, don't you think?"

"Hmm," Jackson nodded. "Reminds me of the taste of those wax lips the kids used to play with at Halloween."

Her face changed.

"I'm sorry," he said quickly. "I didn't mean to bring . . ."

She stopped him. "No, I'm sorry. I'm so sorry to have reminded you."

He sighed. "Everything reminds me. You'd think that being someplace where they had never been, it would be different. But it's not."

"I know," she said.

"I know you do, Livvy." He looked her in the eyes as he said it, but she broke the gaze and looked back at the huffing ocean. It reflected in her eyes, moving.

Why had he thought a walk in the sea breeze would blow away their mood, their pasts, their sorrow? "Lead on," he said lightly, tapping her shoulder.

Livvy turned, bending easily into the climb. He watched her back, following. She had insisted on carrying the backpack containing the picnic lunch, had slapped his hands away both times he tried to take it over. Even now, especially on this incline, she didn't look equal to this kind of physical exertion, so narrow through the waist. Her wrist bones were so tiny, her anklebones. But her breath wasn't even coming hard.

If there was one thing he knew about Livvy, it was that she only looked delicate. He had come to understand that she was like one of those women buried in all the mossy New England grave-yards along the roadsides, the Elizabeth Morgans and Hannah Libbys and Charity Mathers, women who had buried as many children as they had borne, who had worshipped a whimsical and unforgiving god, who had lost their husbands to this same churning sea. Her name, Olivia Faraday, would seem apt, carved in granite, standing next to theirs. Enduring.

When the two of them had walked out far enough on the point, the coast to the north came into view. "Look, you can see Edison Light from here." She pointed toward a distant rocky outcrop on a spit of land where a tall, white lighthouse broke the jagged horizon. "It's one of the most photographed lighthouses in the world."

"You've been reading your tourist brochures again."

"We can drive out there someday, if you want," she said. "It has a lot of history." She tried to look him in the eye, casually, as she said it, but couldn't pull it off. She studied the lighthouse instead.

"Does it?" he said, and wondered what they expected of each other, how much distraction, for how long a time? What was he counting on? What was she?

"I wanted to show you something from up here." She readjusted the backpack. It looked heavier all the time, especially between the little wings of her shoulder blades.

"Let me take that now," he said. "My turn."

"Stop trying to be so chivalrous, Jackson, and enjoy the view."

"I am."

She laughed. "No, I'll bet you're thinking about the light doing this or that to the seawater, or something about the moon and the tide. I want you just to enjoy the view. The beauty."

"I can enjoy it on more than one level," he said, capturing her gaze as he spoke.

The color came into her cheeks. "Come on," she said. "You're slowing me down."

They rounded the tip of the point, and out about a mile from shore a rocky shoal protruded from the sea. On one end, the rotting ribs and masts of a small schooner rested against the rocks. The waves foamed white as they broke over the remains of the deck of the ship. "Eight men lost their lives in the fog the night it went aground," she said. "The whole coastline is littered with wrecks. Sometimes not even that lighthouse up the coast is enough protection in a storm. What can you do when the wind blows you where you don't want to go?" She looked at him, tucking a strand of blowing hair behind her ear.

"Drift with it," Jackson said.

She studied him. "What am I going to do about you?" she said, moving suddenly, throwing her arms out. "Or without you?"

He was startled and swung his eyes to hers, and she held them.

He had grown accustomed to the veiled way in which they spoke, the cryptic communication, double meanings.

"I could ask the same of you," he said.

She nodded. "You could." She looked back out to the shipwreck. "Are we being fair to each other?"

"No," he said. "But life isn't fair, is it?"

"No. It isn't."

Jackson wanted to reach around her waist, pull her close to him so he could bury his thoughts, his conflicting emotions in the sweetness of her hair, the warmth of her pink skin. He sensed she wanted this too, but as much as he told his arm to move around her, it didn't. The wind whipped around them, lashing at the fabric of their jackets.

"Do you think wishing is the same as praying, Jackson?" she said.

"It can be," he said as he stood next to her and watched the sea. "Certainly it involves the same sort of concentrated mental focus on a specific . . ."

She interrupted him. "Because sometimes I wish so hard, it makes my head whirl. I feel it in my blood. It pounds in my ears. I see colors."

"I don't wish," he said quietly. "Not anymore."

"I don't believe that." She looked at him hard. "I don't think you'd be here today. With me. I think this is all about wishing. It's another form, just being here on this cliff together."

He studied an onrushing wave, the way it humped and rolled

and then crested white. "You're right," he said. "I don't call it wishing, though. I call it hoping."

She nodded.

He said, "Trying to see that your future might turn out better than your past, trying to get a glimpse that better is at least a possibility."

"First stars at dusk, falling stars, heads-up pennies, and knocking three times," she said. "I'm into them all. And I don't know why, but it makes me feel like I have some influence, however shaky. You probably think that's crazy. It's not scientific, certainly."

"No," he said. "I wish I could have a little of it, a little of that belief in something, wishing or praying or hoping, whatever you want to call it. There is some science on the matter, believe it or not. People who pray and worship live longer. So they say. Anyway, it can't do any harm."

She said, "Sometimes I'm not sure if I'm wishing for the right thing."

He drew her off the path to sit on the rocks below. Livvy wrapped her arms around her legs and drew them up to her chest. He stretched his legs out, leaned back on stiff arms. The cragginess of the rock felt rough and warm and solid under his palms.

"I needed this," he told her. "I've driven across this country asking myself these questions and giving myself whatever answers I could conjure up. None of them satisfying, at all. What could be?"

"What could be?" she echoed, agreed.

"And it's not that you have the answers, Livvy. I don't expect you to. It's just nice to have someone else asking the same questions, seeking whatever I'm seeking, trying to find a way past the pain."

She nodded.

"It's a pull between us, like electrons spinning around an atom. The result is a balance, like the gravitational hold that keeps the moon from spinning off into space."

"You mean chemistry?" she said. She raised her eyes from beneath her lashes.

He grinned and nodded, looking out at the crumbling shipwreck. The sea washed away the rotting wood splinter by splinter, dissolving the tall masts with wind and salt. In time, nothing would remain of the ship. Memory would fade from generation to generation and all that would be known of the wreck would come from the yellowed fragments of newspaper accounts preserved in libraries and the markings on old charts.

"I thought, Livvy . . ." he said, so quietly that she had to lean into him to hear. "I thought that I had died with them. And for the first time, I'm having feelings that make me feel very much alive." He wanted to wrap himself around her as he spoke. But again he sat still, letting the wind score across his face.

"Part of me," she said, her eyes tearing, maybe from the wind, "part of me feels that, too. But I'm afraid it's a screwy thing, what's happening between us—or trying to happen. Because of what you've gone through, what I'm going through. I'm afraid we're not thinking right?"

"Or hoping right or wishing right?" he said.

"Whatever it is," she said.

"Whatever it is, I don't think you can get it wrong. I haven't felt anything in a long long time, anything good. And I feel you." He looked at her until she looked back.

She nodded. "But I can't name what I feel, Jackson, can't be sure it's all that good for me. Or for you," she said. "And you can't put it in a test tube."

He laughed. "That's all right, even I think this escapes analysis," he said. They were together, and that was enough, talking this way, letting it out. He laid his hand on hers, and she turned her palm into his, pressing. Their fingers entwined. And for many minutes, they just watched the sea washing up and back, watched it foam around the shipwreck and around the rocks on which they sat. They watched the floating gulls fall and rise.

When she finally spoke, he almost didn't hear her over the ocean noise. He wasn't even sure she was speaking to him, maybe only praying out loud, asking, pleading to know. "Just because my husband can't live his life, does it mean I can't live mine?" She asked it in the voice of someone who already knew her answer, who already knew her own sad truth.

Chapter 14

*The laws of nature are the same and the speed of light is the
same in all systems of reference moving relative to one another
at uniform speed. All motion is relative, and measurements of
time, space and mass depend upon the relative speed
between the observer and what he observes.*

EINSTEIN'S THEORY OF SPECIAL RELATIVITY

A white-hot beam of sunlight woke Jackson in the morning and as
he opened his eyes to it, the first thought he had was about Livvy.
He wanted to walk with her again, hike the coastline from cliff to
cliff. He wanted to go there so often that they would know where
every teaberry plant bloomed. They could pack picnic lunches

upon picnic lunches and carry cold lemonade in a thermos. He imagined them spending their days together, one unfolding into the next, the years too. There would be hours browsing through old bookstores, or sitting in dark movie theaters on rainy days. They would drive cross-country. Or follow the old Santa Fe trail on mountain bikes. He'd always wanted to do that. They might sail on one of those giant schooners out of the Rockpoint harbor that slept eight and carried a crew. Or kayak to all the shipwrecks that lay offshore. Or just sit at home and watch each other's hair grow gray. He wanted to go down to her right then, find her standing at the stove over breakfast maybe and slip his arms around her waist from behind, nuzzle her neck, kiss the flesh of her ear.

But in an instant it faded. His heart seemed to flounder. What about Nancy? And the children? Had he forgotten them so quickly? Had he forgotten what he had done in their defense? Jackson let himself collapse back in bed. His head felt feverish. He was ashamed that his mind had grown so reckless. The blood slowed in his veins, grew sluggish with reality.

He tried to picture Nancy in his mind and nearly panicked when all he could see was Livvy. She clouded his mind like thick incense. He felt smothered. He couldn't draw a clear breath.

Going to the window, he opened it to the salty freshness of the air on this edge of the continent. The sun was still shining at a low slant on the sea, and it stretched before him, a shifting sheen. The grass was that green of early morning, each blade seemingly limned in gold. In the flower garden, Livvy was bent over a bed, planting perennials. She worked with her careful movements, and then stopped, seemed to sense his eyes on her. She looked up over her shoulder, smiled to find him really there, watching her. "Good morning," she called.

Jackson waved back, feeling eerily disconnected from himself. "Good morning," he said.

She looked at him quizzically. But he only waved again, reassuring her, and moved away from the window. In a moment, when he glanced again, she had gone back to her planting.

He had to get away. It was plain that he had gotten in over his head. Yesterday she had been right. They weren't being fair to each other, couldn't be. Their thinking had to be warped by pain, like his colleagues' home in Illinois the year of the big floods. The beautiful pine floors had been smooth and honeyed one day, then the waters obscured them, and when it finally receded, there was only mud and under the mud, wood that had swollen and grown dark and warped, as if to mimic the waves of water that had lapped over it, the waters that had mounted higher, changed it forever.

Jackson believed his heart had badly warped. He had proof that it had changed into some dark version of itself, unreliable and murderous. He couldn't inflict himself on Livvy. Whatever he wished for himself, whatever he hoped, he couldn't let her get involved more deeply with someone capable of what he had done. He couldn't.

He had stopped here at the inn for a night's rest and some

conversation, but he hadn't expected to change his life in any way. For Livvy's sake, he had to keep going. For Nancy's and the kids'. He had tended, needed to tend, his family's memory like embers. He carried this as early nomads had carried their fires, carefully, breathing it back into life, sustaining it so it would sustain them. He alone could tend it, and if they were out of his thoughts for even an instant, he might lose them forever. They might turn to charcoal, cold and bitter.

His car, he thought. Escape.

His spirit sank. The Quark was incinerated. Quickly, he dressed and made his way through the lobby. He stood on the front porch and she looked at him from the garden.

"There's coffee inside," she said.

He walked down to her. "That's okay," he said. "I'm going into town."

"Do you need a ride?"

"Thanks, but I'll walk," he said. "I'm going to see about a new truck." It was just something he had to do, and he hoped she would understand. He knew a certain understanding ran in her blood as it ran in his: the unrelenting anguish.

"A new truck," she said. She tried to hide her surprise. Was it hurt, too?

He left quickly, didn't look too closely in farewell. He left her to tend her gardens. She had purple lupine coming up, and columbine, and tulips. She had showed him the beds she had dug on the sunny lawn and the variety she had planted. The gardens had been all that kept her breathing, these past years, she had told him. "Planting a seed is about tomorrow, not yesterday," was how she had put it. When she was bent over the earth, her hands dark with soil, when she took a green seedling onto her palm and shifted it where it could spread roots and grow, in those moments, she was thinking about next spring, next summer, about what might turn out to be a better time. She could forget then that Howard was wearing his pajamas inside out with his face patchy with beard because he had forgotten how to shave right. She could forget herself.

Jackson passed all her spreading hopes as he walked toward the street, toward his leaving. Creeping phlox burned a bright red-pink in feathery explosions. There were fuchsia-colored clusters of dwarf lupine, and a delicate, wispy plant with pale blue flowers the size of the nail on a child's pinkie. He would have to ask her the name of that one when he got back.

They would talk only about tiny blue flowers, about the proper way to boil an egg, about what a fringe of clouds boded on the horizon. He would show her his map and ask advice on the best routes to take up toward Canada, toward the offshore islands, toward somewhere else. They would not talk anymore about wishing or hoping or praying. He would put his hands on the wheel and drive toward tomorrow. She would kneel and plant something to bloom when it came, when tomorrow came.

Walking the shore road, he tallied the money in the bank. He could easily afford a used vehicle without waiting for the check from the insurance company. It probably wouldn't amount to very much anyway for the old Quark. Not like the other check. The one from the life insurance company had made him comfortable enough that he didn't have to work for a long time. But it was no compensation for that loss. None at all. When he had received the life insurance proceeds after the funeral, he had deposited it in their formerly joint checking account, and had since let its balance tick down like the sand in an hourglass.

At the service station in town, he gave the Quark one last good-bye pat on the driver's door.

"I think it's ready for the crusher," said Sammy, who owned the station. His stone face suddenly cracked into a hacking laugh. "That engine's not worth anything now, even for parts."

"It was good while it lasted," Jackson said. He flipped the blue tarp back over the Quark like a shroud.

"You could take the rearview mirror as a souvenir." Sammy winked.

"That's okay, I've got the memories." Jackson smirked.

Sammy broke into a rib-snapping laugh. When he calmed enough, he lit the cigarette pinched between his lips, holding the lighter with both hands to steady a tremor.

"I'll call Yankee Salvage, and they'll pick it up this afternoon," he said, exhaling smoke like an engine burning oil. He coughed hard, worked something around in his mouth and swallowed. "What are you going to do now?"

"Don't know," Jackson said. "That's why I came to you."

"Let me show you what I've got next door."

He followed Sammy to a small lot next to the station. Parked up against one edge of the harbor, next to the back door of the Rockpoint Fish Market, were five cars. You could just see them from the road with red, white, and blue streamers slipped over their antennas. The streamers whipped in the breeze.

"What are you looking for?"

"I haven't thought much about it," Jackson said. Seagulls shrieked overhead and swooped in to pick through the open dumpster behind the fish market.

"Something in a sedan or a sport coupe?" Sammy asked, trying to sound like a smooth salesman. The fact that there were no sedans or sport coupes on his lot didn't seem to matter. Instead, there were three different-sized pickups, a yellow Camaro with a crushed driver's side door, and a huge dump truck.

Jackson looked at the Camaro first, mostly because it chilled him. There was a crack spidered across the windshield where someone's head had impacted. The door was marred by bright blue paint from the vehicle that hit it.

"Low mileage, and it's got a solid engine," Sammy said. "I'd take care of all the body work for you."

"Seems like bad luck to own a car that's been wrecked like that," he said. "Besides, I'm not the kind of guy who drives a Camaro."

Sammy chuckled and the phlegm percolated in his throat. "I know exactly what you mean."

Jackson climbed into the cab of the white Ford pickup. It had an extended cab with a jumper seat where he could keep his photo albums and sketchbook. The bed of the truck was covered with a gray cap with smoked-glass windows.

"How much for this one?"

Sammy shrugged. He cleared his throat again, waiting for Jackson to make an offer.

"How about straight blue book price?" Jackson offered.

"I'd consider it," he finally said, opening his mouth to let loose a burp of a laugh.

There was no bunk to sleep in as there had been on the Quark, but he could always trade the cab in for a camper that would slide into the bed. That way he could pull into any campground and climb into the back for the night.

It occurred to him that he didn't really want to go on like that anymore. Even as he paced around the pickup, appraising it, he thought of those lonely nights where the blood would pound in his ears and blend with the rush of traffic on the road. There were too many mornings when he woke to the squeal of air brakes from the big rigs pulling out, when he spent his first seconds of consciousness trying to remember what state he was in. He'd had enough of those heart-arresting truck-stop breakfasts, sitting in a booth by himself with a plate of eggs and hash browns, hold the bacon. Truckers around him whispered to wives and scolded kids on calling-card telephones clamped to the wall in every booth. Or they argued with dispatchers, rattling the silverware when their fists dropped to the table. But Jackson never had anyone he wanted to call. How long can a man keep moving through life when he's feeling so lost?

"I don't know where I'm going to go in it, but I'll take it," he said to Sammy.

"Don't you want to drive it around the block?" Sammy said. "Take it out on the turnpike. Rev it up. I'll even throw in a dollar for the toll."

"You say you've checked it out," Jackson said.

"Inside and out," he assured Jackson.

"That's good enough for me."

"Let me start her up for you," Sammy said. "I'd feel better about it." He cranked it, then he popped the hood to show off the engine. "Thirty-eight thousand miles. But I have to tell you the inside story. This is my brother's truck. He just had his third kid and his wife told him he better buy something the family could ride in or she would kick him out for good." He howled. "She's got my little brother driving a minivan now."

As Sammy filled out some paperwork, Jackson arranged for payment. He registered the car to his home in Illinois, but he didn't really know where he was going to end up. They shook hands and Sammy lit up another cigarette. He took a long drag.

"You've been friends with Mrs. Faraday long?"

"Long enough," Jackson said.

"She's a good person," Sammy said. "What she's going through . . ." He shook his head.

"I know," Jackson said.

"You wouldn't think a woman like that could tough that out."

"She's tougher than she looks." And as he said it, he hoped it was true. He hoped she was tough enough to withstand everything and his leaving too. He wasn't sure he could withstand it.

Jackson drove his new truck back down to Beach Road, where he idled for a long while at the stop sign before making the turn. He didn't know what Livvy's reaction would be, but he planned to say good-bye quickly. He had to get away. It didn't matter where, but as hard as it was to go, he had no choice. Finally, he shifted into gear and headed back to the inn to pick up his things.

Chapter 15

In some sort of crude sense which no vulgarity, no humor,
no overstatement can quite extinguish, the physicists
have known sin; and this is a knowledge
which they cannot lose.

J. ROBERT OPPENHEIMER (1904–1967)

Livvy circled the truck three times as though she were casting a
spell. Her lips were pinched together, and the fair skin on her
neck, which he could see through the open buttons of her blouse,
was gradually taking on a blush, this one fiery. She pulled her gardening gloves off, gripped them tight in her hand, and slapped
them across her palm. Finally, she dug her feet into the drive so
the gravel crunched like glass.

"So you're leaving?" she asked.

"Thinking about it," Jackson said.

"Well, I can't ask you to stay," she said. "I'm a married woman." She dropped her hands to her hips.

"I'm packed," he said. There was no choice. The rules of attachment had eluded Jackson. Maybe he had simply transmuted into his loneliness, evolved into what consumed him.

"Where are you going?" Livvy asked.

"I don't know," he said. It was true, he was only stumbling blindly along. "Maybe Canada. I thought you might have a suggestion, a nice drive."

She looked at him with her lips parted in incredulity. "Well, what can I say?" She shrugged and folded her arms across her chest, shutting him out as quickly as she could.

"Livvy, I just feel like I have to keep moving," he said. "If I stop, it catches up with me." He didn't want to hurt her, but he could see he was. He wanted to say that she didn't really know him, know what he was capable of. She didn't know what he had done and why he had left his home. It burned in him to tell her that he had blood on his hands and that it had soaked through his skin, had circulated in his body, had stained his heart. "Look, if I don't go, what you're feeling right now you'll feel later, only worse, more intensely. So will I. You were right yesterday. We're screwy. How can we help but be?"

"Well, come back and visit again," she said, not masking the bitterness in her voice, or the tears. "That's what I tell all my guests."

"You have a business that's going to demand everything you have in a few weeks. You have a life that runs without me. And . . ." Jackson hesitated.

"Please," she said, fighting to kept her emotions steady. "You don't have to remind me about Howard. I love him. He's more than my responsibility. He's my husband. I do what I do out of love. Nothing more, nothing less."

"I know. I didn't mean to imply." He moved to take her in his arms. He laid his cheek against the smooth warmth of her hair. She let him for a moment, and then stepped back. "I don't want it to be this way," he said. "Can't we just have a nice lunch together and talk about the name of those tiny blue flowers in your shade garden, and then can't I kiss you on the forehead and say thank you and mean it so much, can't we go that way?"

"Good-bye, Jackson," she said, laying her hands over his.

He stepped up into the white truck and rolled down the window.

She didn't step any closer.

"Livvy," he said.

"They're forget-me-nots."

He was confused. He quizzed her with a quirk of his eyebrows.

"The little blue flowers," she said. "They're forget-me-nots."

She turned and walked toward the house, mounted the steps, put both hands on the railing.

In the rearview mirror as he drove away, he watched her standing there. She grew small and alone. She didn't move.

Jackson drove north in the traffic on Route 1. He was tired of running away. But maybe he didn't deserve anything more. In a universe composed of light and dark, isn't it reasonable to assume that a man's soul has equal qualities? Not just a dusting of each, but both in full force, balancing each other and composing the whole. The brilliance of the stars, after all, is made so striking by the darkness that surrounds them.

Corresponding actions and reactions were the way the universe held itself in balance, and it was the only truth that Jackson trusted. Was he leaving now because he didn't want to forget them—his family—fearing that they would be eclipsed by his own motion, by his going on? Or was he leaving because choosing Livvy—choosing love—would mean not forgetting, but remembering it all? He had told her of the blackness that had engulfed him. But he had not told her of the blackness he caused—a crime all his own.

He wished he could have admitted to her how he had watched over the man. Richard Polk, out on bail, had resumed the activities of his miserable life. And Jackson had built his day around him, moving from bars to greasy cafés. The murderer, Jackson learned from a profile in the newspaper, was a father himself. He had a son, just Nathan's age, who lived with his mother in Pittsburgh.

Polk returned to his job selling restaurant supplies, driving to see his clients. Suspended license or not, he was going to get back behind the wheel. He made no pretense of abiding by the law while he was out on bail until his trial for the "vehicular homicide" of Jackson's family. He had been dead drunk when he collided with Nancy's car. Levi told him Polk was so pickled he could hardly steady himself against the side of his truck to take a piss as the cops finally pulled up to wrench the remains of Jackson's family from their car.

"Trials don't matter," Jackson had told Levi. The deed was done, and it didn't take an Einstein to tell you that you can't turn back time.

The murderer was driving a borrowed car, a tan Camaro that seemed too small for his bulk. Jackson knew he could have him arrested for driving with a suspended license, but what good would it do? Polk's lawyer would have him out in an hour. It made no difference to Polk's customers that he had killed a family. Not one of the restaurant managers on his route refused to buy from him.

"Go on with your life," Levi told Jackson. "Let me take care of things for you."

But Jackson's life had evaporated into a silver thread that traveled into the clouds. He felt compelled to seek out what he could manage, so he took up the trail of the murderer's life. In the awful quiet days after the storm of the funeral, Jackson shadowed Polk everywhere. He parked outside Polk's rented bungalow with the rusted lawn furniture in the yard, and then followed him, unnoticed, as he visited clients, offering pizza ovens, industrial-size dishwashers, or sides of beef. His company provided one-stop shopping for the town of Wendell's fern bars and Mexican restaurants. Polk took their orders, and the company sent a truck out to make the deliveries. Jackson trailed him to the Silver Saddle, Mandarin Mae's, and Casa Grande, places Jackson had eaten with his own family on their nights out. It sickened him to think that their paths might have crossed before. As he and Nancy ordered an early dinner, hold the olives so Nathan wouldn't gag, Polk might have been lurking in the kitchen, belly up to a stainless-steel prep table, tucking into a cheese-shrouded enchilada platter.

After work, as Jackson followed, Polk always stopped at a convenience store for a six-pack or two of beer, and headed home. Jackson watched from his car as the murderer drank himself to sleep alone in front of the colored light of his TV. Polk's puffy face, slack mouth, and watery, piggish eyes were crafted by years of sadness and alcoholism, but Jackson couldn't let himself forget what he had done to Nancy and the kids.

One Friday night, Polk drove to the Rusty Wheel, a bar on his route. The parking lot was crowded with revelers, the night churned, and the lot exhaled pickup trucks and late-model cars in a long steady stream like a sigh. Polk wasn't on a sales call. He was there to drink and get drunk. A drunk at home was a nuisance, but a drunk planning to drive home was a deadly weapon. He didn't come out again until the lot was nearly empty. Jackson was fighting to keep from dozing off.

In the hot white safety lights of the parking lot, Jackson watched as Polk stumbled from the door. He staggered across the gravel lot and climbed into his Camaro. Jackson pulled up beside him and rolled down his window.

"You can't drive in your condition," Jackson said.

"Go fuck yourself," Polk shouted back at him. He stared at Jackson with burning red eyes, and suddenly there was an instant of recognition.

Yes, Jackson wanted to shout, *I'm the one. It's my family you killed in the very same condition you're in tonight. And you could just as easily kill again tonight.* Jackson tried to pull in front of him to block him in, but Polk spun around, driving keenly for a drunk, and took off. Jackson floored his car and followed.

The road back toward town was as straight as the linear particle accelerator he had run experiments on at Princeton, but Polk drove it as though he were driving a winding mountain pass. A passing car hugged the shoulder as he careened into the other lane, gathering speed. Jackson was determined, pounding the steering wheel, shouting out the open window. He cut Polk off where the road made a single right angle into town, forcing him over the shoulder into a dark culvert. He didn't care if either one of them was propelled through the windshield.

Jackson braked hard and steered off the road. He jumped from his car and scuttled down the steep walls of the ditch to the Camaro, which lay overturned. Its wheels still spun in space as the engine sputtered. Polk had climbed from the car, and was steadying himself against it as he touched a single bloody scratch across his cheek.

"You son of a bitch," he shouted at Jackson.

Polk lunged up the embankment to throw a fist that found the hard bones of Jackson's face. Jackson reeled back in surprise. He wobbled for a moment to find his balance and finally dropped to his knees. His fury stole the words from his lips, and he steeled himself against the ground. He tasted the metal of blood in his mouth.

"Fuck you," Polk yelled. "I'll kill you, you goddamn bastard." He stood over Jackson and windmilled his arms with a series of wild, drunken punches to the air.

Jackson felt a darkness eclipse his heart. He rolled away and onto his feet as Polk swung again. The anger exploded inside Jackson and nearly blotted away his reason. There was only bloody rage. He rushed at Polk, who stumbled forward, his black eyes on fire with the challenge. Jackson was still surging ahead when Polk tripped, and he felt him slap his shoulder on the way down. He heard a thud and turned to see Polk lying against the drainage rocks lining the steeply dug slope, his body curled unnaturally as he exhaled a weak groan. Blood from his head ran dark over the jagged spike of pale limestone his skull had impacted.

Jackson stood over the body and felt nothing. There was no sense of relief, or joy, or closure. There was only blood flowing from his nose and a bitter taste in his mouth that made him want to vomit. He climbed the wall of the ditch, ignoring the approaching wail of sirens, and drove home in a cold, wild panic. He was a murderer now too.

Jackson sat at a turnoff on the coastal highway, the radio tuned low to a college station playing a slow John Coltrane saxophone riff, and he tried to summon the strength to get over himself. He thought of the last time he had taken flight, couldn't stop thinking about it. Had he killed Polk in desperate self-defense that night or had he stalked him and murdered him in cold blood? Even Jackson wasn't certain. Whatever it was, Jackson was still responsible. Polk would be alive now and serving out his time if Jackson hadn't killed him.

There had been nothing satisfying in seeing the life that took his family from him extinguished. Revenge was so oddly hollow. There was no resonance or depth to the act, only the pain that it inflicted on Jackson. The truth that haunted Jackson was that he had taken a father away from his son. Polk's boy needed him, no matter how flawed or fractured their relationship. Perhaps they might have salvaged it someday when the boy was older. The boy had just visited for a long summer weekend, before Polk went on his blind binge and killed Jackson's family. Who, Jackson wondered, had to tell the boy that his father was now dead?

A father's love, Jackson knew, flowed inside you, like blood. And children, in their enormous wells of forgiveness, could overlook those tears in the fabric of a father's—or mother's—soul. Jackson knew how much he missed his own father, as imperfect as he had been. There was a comfort in the time that they had shared, and the breakfast eggs they had eaten through the years. The roughness of that male face pressed against his baby-fatted cheek, he had always remembered. The smell of Chiclets and Old Spice when his father bent down to pat his head after he had put his coat and hat away in the hall closet when he came home from work. The pads of eye-ease green ledger paper that he brought forth from his black Samsonite briefcase for Jackson to scribble on with a soft pencil. Jackson had stolen those moments from Polk and his son. For that, he would always grieve.

After Polk's death, he hadn't waited for the sun to rise. The black edge of night was still drawn against the dawn when he locked the house, loaded a few belongings and his precious photographs, and sped away. He drove aimlessly toward Saint Louis, shivering. Maybe it was the cool night air—more likely it was fear, or remorse. In the morning, after a bagel and coffee at a shop on a commercial strip, Jackson traded in the family car for the Quark. He needed some way to be self-sufficient and not have to rely on renting a stucco-ceilinged motel room to get a night's sleep. Like everyone else, he had read Steinbeck's *Travels with Charley* as a boy, and now when he was most desperate it was that form of self-contained travel that beckoned to him.

Jackson believed if he was wanted for murder in one state, he was at risk in all the others. For weeks, he drove only at night, sleeping like a fugitive during the day, bathing in rest stop sinks, eating in crowded truck stops where he could hide out in a booth behind a cup of black coffee. Then he took some chances, staying in a motel occasionally, driving during the day when it was easier, and planning a route that dipped south so he could visit his mother in Florida.

As time passed, he realized he wasn't being followed. There was no all-points bulletin out for him. Once he even ducked into a post office just to see for himself. And there on the wall were a dozen posters of murderers, rapists, and bank robbers, none of which were him. It didn't change his feelings, though. Snuffing out the life of another human being had changed him, made him reticent about public spaces, made his heart race when a patrol car passed him on the highway with sirens blaring, and exposed a streak of paranoia traced inside him like a vein of quartz. For some months, suffering the silence and the solitude of the road, Jackson began to believe that the FBI was stalking him. He suspected that some brilliant tactical team was plotting his arrest from an underground command center deep in the Rocky Mountains. When he realized how ridiculous this was, his guilt returned tenfold, crippling him for days at a time, curling him into a fetal ball of sorrow and regret.

It was worse to get away with it. It was worse.

He hadn't meant to kill him. Or had he? He didn't know. Jackson wasn't violent toward others, and except for a grade-school tussle, he had never even been in a fistfight. The accident that caused Polk to tumble to the ground played in Jackson's memory like a nightmare. Polk had swung first, that's true, but Jackson incited the violence. He chased it down. There was no question he had wanted to see Polk dead, but the moment an angry fantasy becomes unexpected reality is a chilling one.

Polk would have killed again, Jackson was sure of it. There was no question he was drunk, and though traffic was light that night he still might have hit someone at high speed. In those crashes, the drunks always seem to walk away unscathed. Sooner or later, though, the drink would have killed him. Still, Jackson knew he had done the wrong thing. He had panicked and run, when he should have gone to the police. Surely, Levi Bloom could convince a jury that Polk's death was accidental. There was nothing premeditated about it—except that Jackson had been stalking him, that the two of them had argued, and afterward Jackson had fled. He was as guilty as Polk was and that realization ratcheted up his general anxiety.

The only peace he had been granted since those two terrible strokes that had taken everything from him—his wife, his kids, his image of himself as someone ruled by the sensible rules of science—the only peace had come from Livvy. To her, he had revealed his anguish over having to bury what he had loved most. And there was healing in that. He had felt it immediately. He had been frightened by it, true, by its power, by its implications. But he had needed it. How he had needed it. How he still needed it.

There was something more he had to say. Something more he needed from her.

He turned the pickup around. If she could meet his sorrow

with acceptance and show him the direction past it, maybe too she could face his guilt. At least he was ready to admit that he was afraid of his future because of mistakes he had made in the past. He was ready to admit that he didn't want to leave Livvy. Not yet. Not like this.

Chapter 16

In the beginning we should remark that the world is like a globe; whether because this form is the most perfect of all, as it is an integral whole and needs no joints; or because it is the figure having the greatest volume and so would be especially suitable for comprehending and conserving of all things.

NICOLAUS COPERNICUS (1473–1543)

The beach sand was cold and clammy against Jackson's hands. It reminded him of the way Nathan's forehead felt when a fever broke. Nathan had been at the age where he picked up every infection that ran through school. Nancy said it seemed like the kids traded germs like baseball cards. Jackson leaned back on a thick trunk of driftwood. The sky was full of layered gray clouds that passed overhead like traffic. He felt right sitting there, waiting for her.

He knew that he couldn't lose them twice, his family. They would always be with him, filling his head with their years together. But he had to save himself and go on, otherwise who would be strong enough to remember them the way they should be remembered, with joy, with celebration: the way Franny's hair took forever to grow in and they thought she'd always be capped with peach fuzz. Or Nathan's sudden announcement that he wanted to drive a cab for a living. And Nancy knowing just what to say to him to make things right after he'd had a bad day. They would always be with him, going about their lives as though they were still in them, and this brought calm. He wasn't going to lose them again.

Somehow, he felt like one of the wild electrons he had recorded in the lab, pinging through space in search of another unstable element whose orbit it could complete. Gradually, he realized that maybe he had needed this instability, to feel it completely. Every skittering particle in the universe is trying to find that certain place where it is stable and complete in its bonds. Jackson had to find the way to let the electrons orbiting the atoms that made up the molecules, that formed the cells, that created the chemical reactions to work his body and mind, he had taken the time to let these elements find a new orientation.

Walking toward him on the beach was all his hope, and she

was wrapped in her burgundy-colored fleece, walking into the wind. In some way, together they found a fragile emotional stability. He was drawn to her, to the gloss of her hair, to the brightness of her blood showing in her skin, to the way she laughed so naturally in spite of how life had snapped her in half. He was drawn to the part of her that could still go on wishing, and he could not run from her any longer. She made him feel whole again.

"I know we can't be together," he said, standing up when she was near enough.

She stopped, searching him with her eyes. He had never seen them so profoundly green. She said nothing to him and for a moment he thought she was angry. Finally, she simply walked into his embrace. They held each other a long time, more tightly than they had ever dared before. When she leaned away, she took his hand and kissed each finger. She kissed the band circling his fourth finger. Then she held his hand against her heart. "I didn't know what I was going to do without you," she whispered. "I panicked."

Jackson tucked his fingers between hers and lifted her hand to his mouth, touched the skin over her delicate blue veins with his lips. She watched him, the hair blowing into her eyes, whipping. He brushed the strands aside with his fingers and kissed the tender skin beside her ear. The warmth of her made him realize how chill the air had become.

"Come back to the inn," she said. "Winter found us again."

Still, despite the cool air, he felt the springtime as he followed her across the street and inside, as he followed her through the lobby and the dining room and back to her bedroom. The room was small, furnished with simple Shaker antiques, so different from the public parts of the house.

She closed the door between them and the rest of the world.

"Are you sure?" he whispered, wanting her to be sure, wanting her. His lips played with the nub of her earlobe.

She nodded and tilted her head back for his kiss. He pressed his mouth against hers and felt a sigh travel through her into him, into the very heart of him, deep. She held herself against him, clinging as though the force of gravity held her. Tracing the angle of his jaw with her fingertips, she followed with her lips, the lips moving as if in some whisper too faint to make out. He only knew what it said to him wordlessly.

They came to rest on the bed, a large wooden bed with four posts that stretched like open arms into the air. He let his hands flow through her fine hair. It felt like silk against his skin. It took all his effort to pull away. This wasn't right. He needed to tell her first what he had done, how dark was his heart, how imperfect was the only gift he had to offer.

"Livvy, I should . . ." he began, pausing for breath.

She sealed his mouth with a kiss. "Shhhhh," she hushed him. "All I want is this moment right now, right here. That's all."

Their kisses began to build, and he clasped her against him. She ran her hands up under the back of his shirt, stippled her fingernails along his spine. Everything in him yearned toward her. Then she pulled back, found his eyes even as she reached for the buttons and undid them one by one. Jackson slowly peeled off her cotton sweater, shivering to see the narrow torso emerge, the smooth curve, the pearly swell of her.

They lay together, and when he touched her, she arched toward him with an urgency. His fingers brushed the tiny pink nipples crowning her round breasts. He kissed the lightly freckled flushed skin at her collarbones. She clasped her hands around his back. As they moved together, she called his name. "Jackson," she said, in those two musical notes she made of the syllables. "Jackson." His mind hushed to any sound, any thought except for those notes, except for her.

Afterward, they lay back watching the late-afternoon shadows grow darker, watching what happened when the earth tilted away from the sun. He thought of love and heat and the conservation of energy. He imagined that the first law of thermodynamics might just be bent enough to apply to love. "If love," he said to her, "were to behave as energy, it couldn't be destroyed, could it? Only transferred to another."

She murmured sleepily from the soft valley of his shoulder.

"It's just a theory," he whispered.

"It sounds good," she answered.

"I'll experiment a little and see what I come up with."

"Please," she said. "Professor."

He could feel her smiling against him, then felt her face slacken into sleep. He held her, began to drift off himself until in her dreams Livvy's leg jerked and kicked him away.

Chapter 17

*All objects in free fall at the earth's surface have the
same acceleration, and therefore, the weight of
an object, which is the force of gravity upon it,
is always proportional to its mass.*

GALILEO GALILEI (1564–1642)

In forming a scientific hypothesis, it is important to choose the
simplest postulate that best explains a collection of facts. For most
of Jackson's students, formulating a hypothesis was viewed as an
exercise as difficult as bridging the Hudson River with a box of a
hundred wooden toothpicks. And to them proving a theory
required the patience and supernatural dedication of an Einstein.

But Jackson knew it only required taking the right steps at the right time.

The scientific method requires that the process of collecting data be exact, allowing hunches to lead to generalized theories, which in turn form hypotheses. A hypothesis requires tangible proof to become a physical law. Jackson whimsically thought of a few of his own devising: Bodies traveling in opposite directions in the same orbit will collide. Or even: When two bodies attract, only another net force can break their bonds. Or, humorously: A body will continue to fall through space until it runs out of space.

At times, Jackson had wondered at the parallels between the laws of the universe and the laws of the heart. Finding a connection depended on the perspective of the observer. An astronomer won't see much of Earth if he only looks at the sky, an occasional shadow on the moon is all. And he might miss seeing a spectacular comet if he's staring at the wrong part of the universe. Jackson's heart may have been ruled by the same laws that hold the planets in alignment, but too often, he had let his head get in the way. Jackson had been battling nature—his nature. He felt like a witness to events that had a momentum beyond his reach. Life was like magnetism; it moved with a force all its own.

When he woke, she was gone. He found her in the garden wearing only a cotton nightgown. It was just after sunrise, though the light was muffled by a lowering sky. The air was quiet and still.

She knelt in the middle of one of her beds. Frantically, she was picking at her flowers.

"Caterpillars," she said, her tone clipped and tense. She pinched off the caterpillars where she could find them and dropped them in a jar she had filled with beer. "They're voracious. They'll eat everything. Look at this. Just since yesterday." The color was high in her face. His reflex was to reach a hand to her forehead to check for fever.

She showed him a leaf riddled with semicircular bite marks. "They'll wipe everything out. Help me!" She cast a frantic look at him, beseeching.

"What do I do?" Jackson said, kneeling next to her.

"Just what I'm doing."

Jackson reached for the green fleshy caterpillars. They felt like overcooked macaroni between his fingertips. He dropped them into the jar of beer, where they writhed for a moment and then relaxed into an alcoholic stupor.

"Look how dry this soil is," she said. "We haven't had a good soaking rain in days. Whoever heard of no spring rain." Even as he gauged the sky for the chance of rain—almost surely, he decided—she stood up and hurried to the hose to connect a sprinkler. "Make sure you get all of them," she instructed.

He put down the jar of beer with the dead caterpillars and turned to her. "Livvy, is something wrong? This is like gardening with the Green Berets."

Her back was to him. She kept working over the hose connection, finally turning on the sprinkler full force. As it sputtered to life and sprayed, she went around to the garage. When she came back, she was dragging a sack of composted manure.

"Livvy," Jackson said. "At least get dressed. You can't work out here in your nightgown."

"Why not?"

"What happened? Last night . . ."

"Last night . . ." She held up her hands. "Last night, I betrayed my husband. Howard. He's helpless. I'm all he has day in and day out. And I betrayed him. Do you have any idea how that makes me feel?"

"Livvy," Jackson said, moving toward her.

"I let myself get swept up in something," she said. She peeled off her gardening gloves and threw them to the ground. "Damn."

"I'm sorry, Livvy. I'm so sorry." He stepped closer. She flinched at his movement. So he backed off a step. "I should have known better. You said we might be getting it wrong. I knew too. It was me. I should have been the strong one. I should have kept going, should have left you alone. I never meant to do this to you, bring you to this. Oh, please, Livvy, blame me, not yourself." It was his black heart, he knew. It had urged him to yet another crime. And he had willingly committed it. Against her.

She climbed the steps to the house, went inside without looking back at him. And slowly, he walked away, feeling their distance expanding from inches to miles to light-years. Their lives had twisted together the night before, like barbed wire, he realized now. He had done harm to her with an act of love. He should not have let them get so entangled. Passion had made them both act so impulsively, and now, her regrets filled him with a self-loathing that pressed hot tears from the back of his eyes.

He walked toward town. The light was flat, and the day seemed to be accelerating into night already. It was darkening toward a storm. He followed the edge of the harbor. There was a sailboat being lowered into the water by a crane at the docks. He stopped to watch the boat swing slowly through the air, two thick belts of industrial canvas webbing cradling it, leaving the massive keel poking through like a baby's leg from a diaper. A man signaled the crane operator with his hands, and when the boat slid fully into the water, he raised both hands to signal stop.

Beyond the boatyard, on the other side of the harbor entrance, was a long stone jetty that stretched out into the sea like a guiding finger. Jackson walked the length of the large rectangular stones. It seemed a more permanent structure than the opposite jetty, which was constructed from a jumble of jagged gray boulders to protect the beach. Together they formed a calm inlet into the harbor, breaking the chain of waves that swelled across the bay.

A man wearing a grease-stained cap pulled low over his eyes sipped from a bottle jacketed in a paper bag and cast a fishing line into the water. Jackson sat on the end of the stone wall, letting his legs hang over the side, feeling the rough split rock rub his calves. A horseshoe crab, looking fierce and prehistoric, bumped up against a tangle of long tails of seaweed, arched its barbed tail, and then drifted under water.

Whatever connection he and Livvy felt was fraught with grief and longing. Love had been so easy for him with Nancy, the way they had fallen together was natural and had none of this heartache. It had been naive of him to think that the joyful things in life would ever come so easily again. Life was a labor now, as sweaty and filthy as quarrying stone.

Jackson knew well the strange apparitions caused by time. Light takes time to reach the eye from a distant object in motion; it bends, it shimmers, and it fades. Objects trace orbits in the darkness, and as their reflected light travels years through time and space, they continue on their elliptical paths. What reaches our eye, peering into a telescope from some hilltop observatory far from the city lights, is a ghost. Like a photograph, it is only a record of what once was. Anyway, our senses are too imprecise to measure our experiences, and they fail us when we're under siege by our emotions. So we must rely on the ghost images of what appears to be. If the force acting on Jackson's heart was as powerful as it felt, then maybe his emotions, like the refraction of light through water, had distorted what he thought he saw.

He wanted to move onward again and find solace for himself.

Somewhere. Someday. He felt that with Livvy he had at least seen the light beyond the shadow.

The air seemed wet, as if the impending rain were oozing in slowly. He thought of starting back to the pickup, getting on the road, but he turned and watched the fisherman pull a mackerel, slick and blue, from the water. The guy grinned at Jackson as he worked it off the hook and dropped the fish in a white plastic bucket. Jackson managed a smile in return, then refocused his gaze out over the ocean.

He needed to go home. Clearing his name would clear the way to his future, whatever it might be. It didn't matter anymore that he might have to spend twenty-five years locked in a filthy cell. By confronting his guilt he might be able to conquer some of it, or at least soothe it. He was never more wrong in his life than to run as he had. Look at where it had brought him, had brought this woman who had shown him that warmth still existed in the world, that he could still feel it.

His mind needed to consider other things than his own sadness. He had no choice but to leave Livvy behind. After all this time, Jackson realized his journey was just a beginning for him. He had miles to go. He had years yet to travel.

And Livvy, poor Livvy, she was still on her journey too. Distances stretched before her. She had to go. Howard was only the shell of the man she had loved, but now Jackson could see how deeply she still cared. Howard had the same hands. He had the same eyes. And even if he could not remember what devotion he owed her, she could not forget what was due him. She still loved her husband, as Jackson loved his wife. But there was more for her to tend than a memory.

The fisherman caught his limit, and hauled his bucket of mackerel back to his truck. Jackson watched a red-striped racing boat run dizzying circular laps off the beach. The whine of the engine cut sharply through the air.

"I've been driving around looking for you." Livvy was standing behind him. Her eyes were on the boat too.

"I've been here."

She sat down beside him on the cool flat stone. A gull swooped in to pick at a slimy pile of bait the fisherman had left behind.

"I'm sorry, Jackson," she said. "Truly sorry."

"Don't be," he said. "You don't have to."

She curled an arm through his, and they watched the water, the breeze snapping her hair against his cheek. He knew, they both knew the way the hollow-point bullet of grief enters so cleanly, to ricochet off bone and tissue until there's nothing left inside. They knew how skin holds together as everything internal dissolves into quivering pulp. He thought of the effort it took to stand over the graves dug for his family. Getting over the sense that he belonged with them, that had been the cruelest blow. Whether Jackson had curled up into the wormy earth next to his family or not didn't matter; he was living as though he had. But

Livvy seemed to know better than to make his mistake. She just needed to see her husband through, that's all. She was in the midst of her grief, as it stretched from year to year, mourning one teardrop at a time. It seemed excruciating to him.

Still, he couldn't deny that her kiss had breathed life into his body and transformed his grief into something under his control rather than a noose wrapped around his neck. Tragedy had drawn them together. But it would also keep them apart.

"Are you going?" she asked finally.

"Yes," he said. "I'm going back. I have to, if only to explain why I left. My life isn't ever going to be right unless I go back now."

She nodded. "Sometimes going back is the only way we can move forward." She sighed.

"Are you going to be all right?" he asked.

She looked at him with sorrowing eyes. But she nodded. "I just have to remember that this is Howard's illness, not mine. I'll get through it. For him."

"Take care of yourself. Just promise me that."

She smiled. "I will. You reminded me that there are good reasons to come out the other side of this ordeal." She squeezed his arm. "You know, you asked me where I wanted to go, somewhere I'd never been?"

He nodded.

"Greece," she said. "I've never been, and I've always wanted to go. But I had forgotten. I had no reality but this place, this circumstance, and then last night I dreamed about that color blue.

You know that blue they always show in the cigarette ads with Greece as the backdrop. I dreamed of that blue Aegean Sea. And now I can imagine myself on one of those islands surrounded by those ancient ruins and by that color blue."

"I'll remember you that way," he said. "Remembering will be like wishing it for you."

"You believe in prayer now, huh?"

"I'm starting to." He took her hand and kissed its smooth clear skin.

"Maybe we can do this in another life?" Livvy said as the first few raindrops landed around them.

"I'll pray for that."

Jackson drove down the coast. It was a good day for driving, although most people wouldn't consider it so. The rain beat against the window, and the wipers worked frantically against it. Wind shook the truck. But it was absorbing work, driving this way. And the weather made the cab of the truck seem like the most cozy place to be, the safest. Already he loved his new truck, and the way he sat way up above the traffic. The cabin was full of soft, molded shapes, and easy-to-read gauges. As he passed the clam flats and the saltwater marshes on the northern coast of Massachusetts, he decided to name the truck Cygnus after the star.

Jackson had become like Cygnus X-1, a gigantic star trapped in orbit around an unseen companion, which astronomers theorized might be the remains of its long-collapsed twin—a black hole. His orbit revolved around the empty space that was his family. As far as Jackson had come, he was still in their orbit.

He detoured off the interstate and was reminded of his journey north, when he wasn't in such a hurry to get places. He saw a place that caught his eye, a roadside stand that had just opened for the season. He pulled Cygnus into the gravel parking lot of the Clam Box, a summer restaurant on a quiet coastal highway near Ipswich. The place was an authentic piece of fried-clam history, shaped like an upright cardboard box that would come overflowing with golden curls of fried clams. Howard Johnson's frozen fried clams were nothing like these delicate, sweet, hand-breaded strips. Jackson ate a large order and through a haze of tartar sauce he felt the last shreds of his melancholy lift. In spite of what he was doing to his arteries, he was doing what was right for his soul, and that was the first step in learning to be good to yourself.

A strange mixture of nerves and excitement fluttered in his stomach and it was more than a belly full of clams. He dialed Livvy's number from a pay phone at a gas station. Her voice on the machine greeted him, and it calmed him.

"I love you, Livvy," he said to her. "That's all I wanted to say."

He hung up the phone. He had left a photo for Livvy propped on her bedside table. It was the Polaroid that the insurance adjuster had snapped of Jackson standing by the shell of the Quark. He thought maybe that's the way she'd like to remember him.

Chapter 18

*I seem to have been only like a boy playing on the seashore,
and diverting myself in now and then finding a smoother
pebble or a prettier shell than ordinary, whilst the great
ocean of truth lay all undiscovered before me.*

SIR ISAAC NEWTON (1642–1727)

Jackson pulled into his driveway two nights later. He was exhausted. He had broken his trip up with brief pauses, but otherwise, had driven straight through. Now that he knew what he had to do, he was impatient to begin.

His headlights swept across the neatly cut grass to shine on the front of the house and then he sat there with the engine idling.

It looked so perfect, he almost expected to see a sudden light in the upstairs bedroom, Nancy waiting up for him.

The house still smelled the same when he unlocked the door. It was a clean, muffled smell of polished hardwood floors and the sweet, yeasty odor of children. It was a long while before he stepped over the threshold from the top of the front steps. His impulse was to call out and announce that he was home, but he knew there was no one who would answer. Someone had been taking care of the house while he was gone, though. The lawn was cut, the hedges pruned, and the leaves washed out of the roof valleys. Inside the house, the woodwork gleamed. There were no dusty cobwebs hanging from the ceiling as he had expected. The power was still on, though he hadn't paid a bill since he left. He went from room to room turning on lights. Even the antique lamp in the living room that he never had a chance to fix had been rewired. In the kitchen, someone had cleaned out all the food in the refrigerator but left the freezer stocked full.

It was Nancy's cooking that filled that freezer. Homemade ravioli filled with sweet beets and onions, plastic containers of stock that she had boiled from free-range chickens, and tomatoes that she had simmered into thick sauce. There were sweet dinner rolls in a bag in the back, and Jackson wrapped two in foil and slipped them in the oven.

He ran the water in the kitchen sink and washed his hands. He splashed water on his face and dried with a fresh dish towel from the drawer where they had always been. When the rolls were ready, he found them desiccated by freezer burn. He ate them anyway, and they melted in his mouth like a sacrament.

Upstairs, all the beds were made, toys and clothes put neatly away. He wanted to call again for Nathan or Franny or Nancy, but what was the point? He'd wait for them to answer and hear only silence. In the master bedroom, Nancy's favorite afghan was spread across the foot of the bed. It was artificially neat, like a museum exhibit intended to give the impression that the people who had lived there had only stepped out for a moment a century before.

Jackson collapsed on the bed. He was too wiped out to care who was taking care of the house. Anyway, in his state of mind, it wouldn't have mattered to him if he had arrived to a houseful of mice eating through the electrical cords. It was clear that someone still cared for the place that had once given his family so much comfort, but being in that house again, with all its memories teeming in his soul, his emotions felt like they were short-circuiting like that old lamp.

He could have slept in his clothes, splayed on top of the bedspread, but he wanted the comfort of home he had craved. When he crawled between the cool sheets, he realized how much he had longed for the gentle softness of the bed he and Nancy had shared. The cotton sheets were washed and worn into a velvety nap, and he pulled the fluffy comforter up to his chin. The hours they had spent in this bed with the steam-bent maple headboard, reading late into Saturday night, sleeping late on Sunday, making Nathan and Franny. When the kids were babies, they slept between Nancy and Jackson, learning their rhythms in breathing and sleeping. Nancy could roll over and nurse them if they cried out, and Jackson could rock them back to sleep. Lying in that bed was where they had learned to be a family, to protect each other from the world outside. But Jackson hadn't been able to protect them from the worst of the world.

He laid his head back down on the pillow and the pulse of the road slowed in his head. His breathing softened, and he was soon overcome by a deep, dreamless sleep.

When he stepped out of the shower in the morning, Reverend Michael Fitzhume was standing in his bathroom. He tossed a towel at Jackson, who wrapped it around his waist. Fitzhume shook his head. He was dressed in work clothes and a Cubs baseball cap.

"I thought that truck had to be yours," he said. "You're just in time to help me finish mowing your lawn."

"So you've been keeping the place up?" Jackson said.

"I can't take all the credit. Millie, my housekeeper, comes once a week to dust and water the plants."

"I don't remember leaving you a key." He reached for another towel to dry his hair.

"You didn't have to," Fitzhume said. "The boys in my parish in Chicago taught me a little of their trade."

"Oh," Jackson said, not knowing whether to be grateful or

annoyed. He grabbed for clothes still packed in his bag and dressed, deciding that he had no right to be anything but grateful. "Thank you."

"That's what friends do," Fitzhume said, tersely. He watched Jackson for a long while. "I guess you know Polk's dead."

Jackson nodded as a bolt of nerves shot through his stomach.

"It happened the night you disappeared." Fitzhume arched his eyebrow as he fixed his blue eyes on Jackson. They were like too rounds of sky staring at him—like the eyes of God, himself.

Fitzhume's belly was rounder, and his fair skin seem to flush more easily with the currents of blood that filled the broken capillaries in his bulbous nose, but he still knew how to play Jackson. He snorted to break the tension and slapped Jackson on the back. "I knew you'd come back home when you were ready. Let's have some coffee and you can tell me where in Saint Saviour's name you've been hiding out."

Fitzhume said he had a box of doughnuts in his car, and while he went out to get them Jackson made coffee in the kitchen. He felt a piece of paper in his shirt pocket and reached for it. It was Livvy's note, left for him the first morning to explain that she had to be away. He let his eyes follow the delicate loops of her handwriting. The crisp paper crinkled in his fingers. He imagined how carefully she must have chosen it. Maybe she had found the sheets browsing in a specialty store on a rough cobblestone street in the old section of one of those coastal towns he had passed through in Maine. He wanted to hold her again, silently and tenderly. He craved those feelings of hope and comfort they had shared in being together.

"Coffee ready, yet?" Fitzhume called as he walked back in the kitchen.

Jackson folded Livvy's note and slipped it back into his pocket. "Almost."

"So what's going on?" Fitzhume asked. It was more a demand than a question. Fitzhume had always struck direct blows when he was impatient for answers.

"The chasm principle," he said.

"The what?"

"My own invention to explain the gap that separates us from the things that make our lives run right."

Fitzhume ran his fingers through his thick white hair and shook his head with great disappointment. "My patience ran out months ago, Jackson," he said, his voice resounding with the power of the pulpit. "You know I don't play games. So don't make me. You went away with not a word, and it made me dizzy with fury. People confide in me a hundred times a day, why didn't you let me help you?"

"I couldn't," he said. "I had to run and try to bridge that chasm. But it only led me right back here." Jackson brought a hand to his forehead. Fitzhume already knew what had happened that night. "I was just thinking of science, that's all."

"Science!" he spat. "Science doesn't explain what happens in here!" Fitzhume pounded his chest. His cheeks took on the ruddiness of an apple skin. "I've looked into the dead eyes of men who had no remorse for their actions. I've heard death row confessions without flinching. You could have come to me, Jackson."

"I know," Jackson said, quietly. "But sometimes a man doesn't need a confessor. I just needed time to make things right in myself."

Fitzhume let out a great gasp of a sigh and brought one of his meaty, rough hands down to his thigh with a slap. He shook his head. He turned once, and then reeled around again, shuddering with emotion, searching for the words he wanted. Finally, he jumped up and splashed coffee into two mugs and pushed one toward Jackson.

"I don't want to say you owed it to me," Fitzhume said. "But we've both lost something here. And then to think I lost you . . . Of course I prayed, but God doesn't give straight answers or forwarding addresses."

"I'm sorry," Jackson said.

Fitzhume snorted, and he reached over to pinch off half a powdered sugar doughnut. He washed it down with a mouthful of coffee. "I can guess what happened that night, Jackson." Again, he arched an eyebrow. "Revenge is not man's to claim."

"Don't preach to me. Not now."

"That's like telling me not to breathe," Fitzhume said.

"I wasn't plotting revenge that night," Jackson sputtered, feeling the cords of emotion tugging at his voice. "I was shattered."

"It's intent, Jackson," he said. "Nothing more than intent concerns me."

"But after what he'd done to them . . ."

"Making a public spectacle of yourself now won't bring them back," Fitzhume said, folding a sturdy palm over Jackson's hand. "You simply have to make peace and go on."

"That's all I want to do," Jackson said, his voice unsteady. "So let me get there the only way I know how." It was with Livvy that he had learned to see outside himself. She had shown him that grief could be channeled, melded into the steady pursuit of purpose. He knew from Livvy that acceptance of his responsibility and pain was the only way he could hope to resume life among the living. He might never be whole, but now he felt like he knew where the pieces were.

"Are you here for them? Or because of Polk?" Fitzhume leaned forward at the table, resting his weight on his wide forearms.

"I came back for me," Jackson said.

The next morning, he found Levi Bloom in his office. It was early and he was alone, away from the chatter of clients and his legal secretary. He was using the tip of a pencil to excise the raisins from a bran muffin and pushing them aside onto a copy of the university's alternative newspaper spread out in front of him.

"Levi," Jackson called.

Levi jumped and nearly spilled herbal tea all over his desk. "Holy shit! Jackson Tate, the man who disappeared without a trace."

Levi wiped his hands on a napkin and came around to shake his friend's hand. He pulled Jackson into a brief, awkward hug.

"How the hell are you?"

"Okay." Jackson slipped into one of the worn, secondhand leather club chairs parked in front of Levi's desk.

"Okay? That's all you have to say? What has it been? A year?"

"Almost." Jackson sighed. He couldn't hold it back anymore and the words tumbled out of him. "I came here to tell you I killed him, Levi."

"Whoa, let's put on the parking brake here for a minute." Levi got up from his chair and closed his office door tight. "Now what the hell are you trying to say?"

"I let Richard Polk die that night and then I left town," he said.

Levi leaned on the edge of his desk and stared hard at Jackson. "Wait, wait, wait," he said. "Richard Polk was drunk the night he drove off the road. Blood tests showed he was a six-pack past the legal limit. The impact threw him clear. When he landed in the ditch, his neck was broken. That's the official version, the unofficial version, and everything in between."

"I don't want this covered up," Jackson said tersely. "I did it. I should serve time or be put to death or whatever this state does to murderers. I can't run anymore."

Levi took another sip of tea. "Just relax for a second, okay? Can I get you something? Tea? Juice? Lethal injection?"

"Don't make light of this," Jackson said. "Do you understand what I'm trying to tell you?"

"Sure," Levi said. "I tried to get in touch to let you know everything was cool. I expected the guilt would catch up to you sometime. I know you, and I didn't want you turning yourself in to the FBI. Who else have you told about this?"

Jackson thought of Fitzhume, but their conversation was as private as if it occurred in the darkness of the confessional. And he thought of Livvy, but he had kept her out of it, and never told her the dirty, incriminating details. All she knew was that he had to get back home to sort out his life. "No one else knows."

"Good, because if you knew the favors I owe to make your name and Polk's go in two separate directions over this thing, you wouldn't do anything to blow it."

"Levi, I'm prepared to face the consequences. I can tell you exactly how Polk and I fought, how he swung at me, how he fell backwards into that ditch and I left him there to die."

"What you just told me," he said. "I could argue self-defense fifty different ways. What's really going on?"

"I'm responsible for ending his life, just as he killed . . ." Jackson slouched back in his seat and brought his hands to his face. "He killed them and I was just trying . . ."

"You were tailing him, waiting for him to get drunk and climb

into his car again," Levi said. "A witness outside the bar said someone was following him. You, I presume."

"What do I do, Levi? Maybe I'm free from the law, but not
myself."

"Trying to get yourself thrown in jail won't change that," he
said. "I was looking out for you because I'm one hundred percent
positive that I could have gotten anything thrown out of court."
He leaned across the desk toward Jackson. "Look, I don't know
anyone who deserves to live a happy life again more than you. And
I know that's how everyone in this community feels."

Jackson was shaken. He had expected to be led from Levi's
office in handcuffs by the chief of police himself. He had confessed to a deed that tormented him, that drove him away from
his home and his friends, and no one wanted to pay attention.
There was no resolution that satisfied him. Was there nothing that
would cut through the muzzle around his heart?

"Isn't it hard enough that they're gone?" Levi said. "Why do
you want to do this to yourself? Tear yourself up like this? Forget
it. Richard Polk was a drunk, he always was, always would have
been. All you did was hurry along the inevitable. Call it a public
service."

"A public service? Levi, he had a son."

"Jackson, you're taking this too far."

"Am I?"

Levi reached over and flipped through the pages of his desk

calendar. "Let's go somewhere and talk about this. I'll call Kate, she'll get a sitter for the kids, and the three of us can get some dinner tonight."

"Can't do it," Jackson said. He edged out of his chair and headed for the door.

"Well, how about tomorrow?"

"I'll let you know," Jackson said and closed the door behind him. He had to do what made his heart right.

The district attorney called for a grand jury hearing as soon as Jackson turned himself in. Levi was at Jackson's side at a long table in a small, cramped courtroom. They faced a group of men and women who made up the jury. In the room, there was a low murmur of conversation under the bass drone of a nearby air conditioner that sent soft waves of vibration across the surface of the water in the glass pitcher on the table in front of him.

"Look, Jackson, we're going to have to use everything we have here," Levi whispered to him. "Remember this isn't a trial, just a way for the D.A. to determine from a jury hearing if he has cause to charge you officially with a crime. But this is an emotional case, and if you feel like you need to emote when you give your statement, do it. That will do a lot to establish what your state of mind was that night."

"I won't cry on cue, Levi," he said. "I just want to tell them what happened."

Levi looked up from the notes spread out in front of his briefcase. "That's what we're here for, isn't it?"

The district attorney, Marty Reynolds, was a corpulent man
who groaned with effort as he pushed himself up from his chair
and stood to question Jackson. He was the one who had charged
Polk with a minor grade of homicide and then had bail set just low
enough for Polk to walk out of jail. Reynolds had a thatch of gray
hair that was carefully layered in place and his shoes squeaked as
he paced in front of Jackson.

"Mr. Tate," Reynolds said at one point, resting his hand on the
dark, lacquered wood of the table. "Stalking Richard Polk, forcing
him off the road, and engaging him in a deadly fistfight, that's not
like any barroom tussle I've ever known. Did you follow Richard
Polk with the intention of killing him that night?"

"I was angry at him," Jackson answered. "I was certainly venge-
ful. How else would I feel? He killed my family and as prosecutor,
you let him walk out of here." Out of the corner of his eye, he saw
Levi cringe.

"Please, just answer the question, Mr. Tate," Reynolds said.

"No, it was never my intention to kill him. Maybe I wanted to
prevent him from killing someone else on the road."

"Because he was drunk?" Reynolds asked. "And because you're
such a good citizen?"

"Well, in a way, yes," Jackson said. "I think that . . . I know that
my reason for stopping him that night was because he was too

drunk to drive. And when he began to assault me, with words and his fists, I just couldn't hold back. My anger took over." Jackson fiddled with the tight knot on his tie and turned in the direction of the men and women of the jury. "In Newtonian physics, bodies react with an equal and opposite action. And that night, that's all I was doing, reacting."

"Sounds almost biblical, like the Golden Rule," Reynolds said with sarcasm.

"I guess it is in some way," Jackson said, trying not to react. "At least to me. After what he did to my family, I don't know how I could have behaved any differently."

After the lunch break, there was testimony by the medical examiner and several police officers before the jury was ready to deliberate. When the day was over, Jackson followed Levi into a dark tavern across the street from the courthouse. They had arranged to meet Fitzhume there. And they found him waiting in a booth with a pint glass of beer in front of him. They slipped in around him and ordered.

"I think it went well," Levi said mordantly to Fitzhume. "The D.A. may actually charge Jackson with murder. "

"You know that's not what I want," Jackson said.

"You're not leaving them any choice." Levi pulled the knot of his tie open like a rip cord.

"I'm prepared to accept whatever they want to charge me with."

"Father, have you ever seen a bigger martyr?" Levi snapped.

"Well, actually, I do know of one other . . ."

"I'm not trying to be a martyr," Jackson interrupted.

"Jesus Christ," Levi groaned. "The way Reynolds was prodding you, he can't wait to get hold of you in open court and gut you. I've seen this before. You have to be ready for this to go south, Jackson."

"I can't change what I've done."

"Of course not," Levi said. "But you don't have to roll over and take a beating. Some of the things you said today blew a lot of holes in your case."

"Enough," Fitzhume boomed. "You're his lawyer. You can't condemn him for taking a moral stand. You should be right there with him the whole way."

Levi took a long draft from his beer. "I know."

A reporter approached the table boldly with his notebook open in his hand. "Any comment on how it went today?"

Levi pounced. "We're not ready to comment until the grand jury comes back."

"Is it true that you planned Polk's murder in advance, Mr. Tate?" the reported asked.

Levi pushed himself to his feet and faced the reporter. "It wasn't murder. In all my years as a lawyer, I've never seen a clearer case of self-defense."

"Easy, Levi," Fitzhume said. He pulled Levi back into the booth. The reporter backed away into the shadows of the bar.

By the time the grand jury did return, Jackson was sure he had made a mistake. Was it really courage that had forced him to return to Wendell and admit to what he had done, or had he just been tired of running? He didn't know. But in the time that had passed since he had left Livvy, he knew how often he had wanted to reach out to her. He missed her reason, her perspective on life, and her kindness. He had never needed anything more.

The grand jury ruled that Polk's death was accidental and that Jackson could not be charged with anything more than reckless driving. Reynolds waved the charge away with a flap of his hand. And in the hushed room, Jackson sat stunned as the jury filed out.

"That's it," Levi said. He lay a hand flat across Jackson's back. "We're done."

"But I confessed." From the hallway outside, Jackson could hear Reynolds addressing reporters.

"No one here thought you did anything wrong," Levi said. "Go home, start your life again."

Fitzhume came in and sat down next to Jackson. He looked at him for a long while.

Jackson shook his head. "They let me go."

"There's such a thing as justice, Jackson, and you ought to accept it when it comes your way," Fitzhume said. And then he took Jackson home.

The jury's verdict conspired against sleep, and Jackson lay there in the darkness of his bed, restless and angry. They had ignored the forensic evidence, and his confession hadn't meant a thing. Why had they let him go? They could have recommended he be charged with manslaughter at the very least. But they hadn't.

He wasn't a martyr. Jackson had only thought that surrendering himself to justice might bring some peace to him. In trying to take responsibility, he thought he could be healed. All he had wanted was to repair the schism that had torn his life apart. But it hadn't worked that way. Whether a jury ruled Polk's death accidental or murder wasn't what really mattered. Jackson's torment was that he thought he had killed a man, nothing more. Paying for his crime was the only way he knew how to settle the storm within himself.

Jackson tossed and then rolled over on his side. He was more restless than he had ever been when he was running away from his deed. His mind raced like a car out of control, spinning out in his emotional exhaustion.

And then he felt it. A tiny warm hand laid against his face. The smell of powder and No More Tears shampoo. He thought he felt a droplet of water fall on his cheek as though it were shaken from Nathan's still damp hair. He heard a giggle from Nathan, and he thought of his playful romps on his way to bed after a bath. His body shining and flushed, warm from the bathwater and smelling clean and sweet from soap. He felt that small warm, moist hand on his cheek so clearly in the darkness, so soothing. His chest felt filled with a delicate glow that calmed him. And then it was gone.

"Nathan," he whispered into the air.

There was no answer. The only sound that broke through the

night was a muffled hum as the refrigerator cycled on in the kitchen downstairs.

The smell of coffee brewing woke him up. Fitzhume had broken in again and brought bagels. They sat together in the quiet morning, listening to the buzz of the heat bugs on the dewy lawn. Summer was nearly over. The year had come full circle since the accident.

"I don't have the answers," Jackson said. "I can't explain my heart."

"None of us can," Fitzhume said.

"They still have a hold," Jackson said. "Since they've been gone, things have happened outside the laws of physics." He paused long enough to gaze out at the rope swing hanging from the low branches of a sycamore in the backyard. It seemed frozen in the calm air. "I felt Nathan touch my face last night. That's impossible, isn't it?"

"Is it? You're the man of science." Fitzhume smiled.

"Don't give me that."

Fitzhume shrugged. "Forgiveness comes to us in many ways, my friend."

This time Jackson decided to accept it.

Epilogue

Jackson's life soon returned to an orbit of its own. He chose to spend much of his time alone, letting the jagged edges of his wounds knit together. But there were occasional outings with Fitzhume, and Levi had him over to his house for dinner at regular intervals. It wasn't easy, though. Fitzhume had his congregation, and Levi Bloom had his wife, Kate, and two lovely daughters. Jackson had himself.

Now that he had been able to put his crimes behind him, he sometimes found a certain pleasure in being alone. He missed his family every moment, of course, but the grief had mellowed into a dull ache that he could surmount with meaningful activity. Today he had found just such respite. He had finished a new painting that afternoon and was savoring the satisfaction of creation and completion. Also, he had been anticipating the solace of a meal at his favorite restaurant, specifically the grilled salmon with rosemary, the familiar potatoes. And then, suddenly and with no expectation that it would ever come at all, there had been the postcard in his mailbox.

The kitchen at Plant 609 was opened to the dining room, and he could watch the frenzied activity as the chef called waitresses over by name to pick up their orders. It was like dinner theater set around a wood-burning grill. He knew Livvy would have enjoyed it too, and it surprised him—thrilled him—to think so casually of her. But he could now. Suddenly. He had license, held her postcard in his hand, could rub its deckle edge with his fingertips as proof, as reassurance. It had been so long since he had allowed his mind to settle on thoughts of her. She had become merely a touchstone. In his worst moments, for consolation, he occasionally indulged the fleeting memory of her—a momentary remembrance of her working at the window box, the look of her face when the ocean was reflected in her eyes, her fingers on his skin. But then he forced himself on to other matters, practical matters. He dealt with all his obligations.

As his last act as Jackson's attorney, Levi Bloom had found Richard Polk's son, Steven. He and his mother were still living in Pittsburgh and they had inherited nothing but the debt of burying Polk. Jackson asked Levi to draw up the papers that would establish a trust. Steven Polk would never want for school supplies, a warm meal, or new clothes. Levi would explain to them that the trust was funded by one of his father's business associates. A son shouldn't have to pay for the sins of his father.

Back home in Wendell, Jackson felt that something had changed inside of him, irrevocably, and until he determined what it was or how to live with it sensibly, he had to let himself experiment. That way, he might learn from his mistakes. There was no doubt that he would return to physics again. It was in his mind like memorized poetry. And he did have new ideas for making the rigid complexities of the laws that ruled the universe more understandable to his students. Perhaps he had even grown to understand them better himself. But for now he needed to look at the whole instead of just atoms.

His fascination turned toward the art that had once only served his science. Soon after moving back home, he had traveled to the Art Institute of Chicago to see just how it was that the great painters used light and shadow on their canvases. He knew about the waves and particles that composed light, but too little about the play of it on the world. At a studio school, he began to master the techniques he needed to expose the light and dark of his own heart.

In some time, he had amassed a collection of work that confidently revealed what he thought he could never see for himself. He did several paintings where danger seemed to taint an otherwise simple family scene. In another, a farmhouse, painted in bold circus colors, lorded over a landscape that had atrophied. And there were many drawings of a coastal inn cloaked in isolating fog and other studies of a woman walking alone on a long stretch of beach.

While his work deeply pleased him, it did not sustain him financially. He exhibited at group shows, and if an offer was made for a painting or drawing, he would not accept it. He wasn't ready to let them go. She hadn't seen them yet.

Jackson hadn't forgotten about Livvy. He had only let the time pass. Her unexpected postcard made him hope that maybe now, fate and time would be better collaborators. As he ate his dinner at Plant 609, his thoughts turned to Livvy. He had only to gaze at her postcard with a picture of an island in the blue Aegean to know that more was possible. She had found the color blue of her dreams, had found herself there, in its midst. Whatever else had befallen her, she had still found her way into her own dreams. Tracing the lush strokes of her pen with his fingertip, he felt the pieces of the earth knit whole again under his feet. He saw the same colors she saw, the same possibilities for beginning anew.

Dear Jackson,
Can a lifetime start again? I've missed you.

Livvy

And in small letters at the bottom of the card, she wrote that she was staying on a Greek island with a name magical to pronounce: Mykonos.

He remembered how he had first seen her bundled into fleece and bright against the gray of the Maine shore, the way they had found each other, alone with their secret pain. She had been lovely to him in her fragility and also in her resolve. In the time apart, the memory of her tenderness had moved him often. His mind would work over her words, following them like the loops and curls of her handwriting. He would analyze and ponder his next steps. He would go carefully, all the while wondering at this one proven thing, at this one thing in which he could believe: He did not have to run anymore.